FIRST GIFTS OF LOVE

Jack was waiting for her by the giant elm tree. "Happy Birthday," he said. "This is for you."

She took the package, neatly wrapped, and opened it. Inside was a velvet box perhaps three by four inches long. Carefully she lifted the lid and peered into it. There, on the cushion, was a tiny gold locket on a gold chain. The locket was heart-shaped and by squinting she could see two sets of initials: J.E. & C.L.

"Jack, it's beautiful," she breathed. "Oh, but you shouldn't have. What will people think?"

"Well, you don't have to show it if you don't want to. If you're too shy, just wear it under your . . . next to your heart. And think of me. You must know how I feel, Charlotte. I want you to be my wife."

Swiftly, before she was aware of what was happening, he drew her into his arms and brought his mouth to hers. It was the first time she had been kissed by a man. She was frightened and she struggled slightly, but he held her firm. The sensation was not unpleasant, she knew she could even enjoy it if she let herself. But something within her pulled her away, told her to run. Abruptly, she tore herself from his tempting embrace and started up the path to the house. . . .

ATTENTION: SCHOOLS AND CORPORATIONS

PINNACLE Books are available at quantity discounts with bulk purchases for educational, business or special promotional use. For further details, please write to: SPECIAL SALES MANAGER, Pinnacle Books, Inc. 1430 Broadway, New York, NY 10018.

WRITE FOR OUR FREE CATALOG

Pinnacle Books, Inc.
Reader Service Department
1430 Broadway
New York, NY 10018

If there is a Pinnacle Book you want—and you cannot find it locally—it is available from us simply by sending the title and price plus 75¢ to cover mailing and handling costs to:
Please allow 6 weeks for delivery.

―― Check here if you want to receive our catalog regularly.

Linton Park no. 1
Charlotte
by Hilary Desmond

PINNACLE BOOKS   NEW YORK

This is a work of fiction. All the characters and events portrayed in this book are fictional, and any resemblance to real people or incidents is purely coincidental.

LINTON PARK #1: CHARLOTTE

Copyright © 1981 by Lee Hays

All rights reserved, including the right to reproduce this book or portions thereof in any form.

An original Pinnacle Books edition, published for the first time anywhere.

First printing, April 1981

ISBN: 0-523-41062-X

Cover illustration by Emerson Terry

Printed in the United States of America

PINNACLE BOOKS, INC.
1430 Broadway
New York, New York 10018

LINTON PARK #1: CHARLOTTE

CHAPTER ONE

Miss Charlotte Linton, on the occasion of her seventeenth birthday, was feted by her family and friends at Linton Park. It was a beautiful spring day, the kind of day found so often in Suffolk in May and June. The party, was held therefore, as much out of doors as inside the huge, comfortable rambling manor house that was set high on a hill overlooking Henry Linton's land (or a considerable amount of it) as well as the road that led from Bury St. Edmonds to Newmarket.

To say that both family and friends were present is somewhat misleading for, in truth, nearly all of her friends were also related to her if only by the most distant of connections, a fact that was not uncommon in that area of pastoral beauty where the rolling gentle hills were so rich that the land could be used to graze cattle, raise grain, and still lie fallow much of the time. Meadows of sweetlark and wild flowers of all sorts spotted the countryside. With so much beauty and with the possibility of sustaining a family so likely, it was not surprising that few people left the Suffolk countryside for greener pastures (there were none) and that, therefore, it seemed that everyone was related, if only by marriage.

The Lintons were among the best-off of all their neighbors, yet they were by no means rich. Henry Linton owned considerable acreage and it was farmed, yielding well, but farm life is not always profitable, and in addition to his several hundred acres, Linton had to keep up a very large house, for he and his wife had eight offspring, six girls and two boys. Charlotte, whose birthday it was, was the oldest girl, the second oldest child.

Then, too, the tenants who worked the land were Henry

Linton's responsibility as well. He was a generous man and no one ever went hungry. Because it was not in his heart to be frugal or callous, the end of the year often found him in tight circumstances, but he had boundless faith, was of a cheerful disposition, and trusted in the Lord to whom he prayed regularly on Sunday. His wife Margaret was of equally good disposition, although she was not outgoing in the way her husband was. The Linton children (and often their cousins) were surrounded with love and happiness and enough of the world's goods so that any of them old enough to be queried on the matter would respond quite openly that theirs was a good, full, happy life. Of them all, Charlotte was perhaps the sunniest in manner.

Fortunately her birthday fell on a Sunday and by late afternoon the house was full, that is, fuller than usual, for it was a rare day when, in addition to the Lintons (ten altogether, although Arthur, the eldest, was away at sea, an ensign in His Majesty's Navy), there were not four or five more at any given meal. Margaret Linton, even with several hired girls and the help of her own older children, still spent considerable time in the kitchen.

The girls, along with their cousin Dunreath Ellicott, were in the large main room, playing Blindman's Buff, a favorite of the twins, especially Rosemary who, since the age of two, when she came home (after being missing most of the day) carrying an armload of wild flowers that she had picked, had been called Posie. The other twin, Elizabeth, was blindfolded, playing "it," and was complaining that she couldn't find anyone and she was sure they had all left her in the huge room and she was afraid. In this, as in most emotional things, she was the direct opposite of Posie, her twin. Only in looks were they totally similar. Still, it was easy for the family to tell them apart for Posie's hair was of a reddish hue, not so blonde as Beth's. Indeed, all of the Lintons, with the exception of the second son, George Henry, now thirteen, were fair. G.H., as he was called, had dark hair and eyes and browned quickly in the summer while the others were blue-eyed and freckled if they got too much sun.

Finally, because she could see that Beth was near to tears, Dunreath Ellicott allowed herself to be caught. Dunreath was the same age as Charlotte and was first cousin to the Lintons, her father and Margaret Ellicott being brother and sister. Just as the Linton girls were all fair, Dunreath had handsomely lustrous, black hair and eyes so brown that they seemed almost black, contrasting a pale, pale complexion. Since the age of five Dunreath had been in love with Arthur Linton, and even though he was now away, she still spent as much time at Linton Park as she did in her own home, Dunreath Manor, some twelve miles away in the direction of Bury St. Edmonds. As she and Charlotte were the same age, they were especially close; but she was fond of all of the Lintons and they, in turn, all loved her, for Dunreath was perhaps the gentlest, kindest person any of them were ever likely to know. She had no sisters of her own, but two brothers, one older and one younger, and so she was thought of and treated as a sister by all of the Linton girls.

Anne Linton, who was sixteen, and the most practical of the girls, decided she was tired of the game. "Let's stop. It's almost time for tea. And that delicious cake. Charlotte has to blow out the candles and make a wish. Besides, Dunreath was 'it' once already."

"I'm going out," Caroline declared. At fourteen, she had suddenly decided that she was a grown-up and she took part in what she referred to as "childish pleasures" only under duress. At this point in her life she wanted to be like her cousin, Alfred, Dunreath's younger brother and now she was anxious to see what he and G.H. were doing. Boys, in her opinion, were more mature than girls.

Her younger sister, Ellen, squealed, "I'll go with you."

"No you won't. Can't a person do anything alone? I don't want a baby . . ."

"I'm eleven . . ."

"That's practically a baby. . . . following me around." With that Caroline went out of the room and ran down the hall to the open door that led to the wide lawn. With the game over, the others began to make plans of their own. Ellen, never daunted, joined the twins. Charlotte, Anne, and Dunreath went toward the kitchen to see if they could help their respective mothers and if it would soon be time to cut the cake.

Margaret Linton and her sister-in-law, Judith Ellicott were close friends. In a way this was odd, for they were quite different. Judith Ellicott was born a Dunreath and she had inherited Dunreath Manor shortly after she married George Ellicott. George, like his sister, Margaret, was country born and bred and had no real desire to spend any amount of time in the city. Nor could he before his marriage, have afforded it, for though he was well-off by Suffolk standards, his money would not have lasted long in London. His wife, however, was rich. Not only had Dunreath Manor and all the land become hers and thus theirs, but she had capital aplenty invested for her in the city and she had inherited a house in Mayfair as well. She had spent approximately half of her life in London returning every few months or so to Suffolk, and she intended to continue to do so even after she married. Her husband went along—but somewhat reluctantly.

She had stuck to that schedule for the twenty-two years of her married life, although George Ellicott often found reasons for not accompanying her—or at least waiting a few weeks before he joined her in Mayfair. Judith was one of those rare people who was equally at home in city or country. She knew all the right people in London and had more invitations than she cared to accept; she had elegant clothes and was considered attractive; and those who did not know her quite often mistook her age by as much as ten years in her favor, thinking her below thirty rather than nearly forty. For all her money and position she could never be considered a snob. She cared much too much for people and she loved the country life as much as the balls and parties of the city. It was her temperament that her daughter Dunreath had inherited, but unfortunately not her constitution, for Judith Ellicott was as healthy a woman as one was likely to meet while Dunreath was often ill. No one could understand why, for George Ellicott was a blusttery, hearty man and both of his sons were equally so. Only Dunreath seemed susceptible to all the diseases that were contagious, and on several occasions the family had despaired of her life.

Judith and Margaret were examining the decorations on the cake when the three girls trooped into the kitchen.

"Mother—Aunt Judith, it's beautiful." Charlotte walked around the long kitchen table, examining the cake from all sides. It was three-layered and quite wide for it would have to feed several dozen people. On the top of the white icing the cook had put a pink frosting of letters that spelled out

Charlotte's name, Happy Birthday, and the date, May 14, 1811.

The girls asked if they could help but they were assured that at the moment there was nothing for them to do, and then Aunt Judith suggested that they go outside and enjoy the fresh air. It was apparent to them that they had interrupted a private conversation and so they left quickly.

The lawn was crowded. Henry Linton was telling a group of four men, including George Ellicott and his nineteen-year-old son, Jack, about some grouse shooting he had done on *his* seventeenth birthday, many years before. The upshot of the tale was that he had bagged his age and had resolved after that never to hunt grouse again, for as he said, "By now I'd have to hit forty-five of the beggars." Everyone chuckled suitably and after the laughter died down, he added, "It was my father who warned me. Always quit when you're ahead, he told me. That was when I wanted to go to a gambling house in London—we visited there once a year—and I was sixteen at the time. Well, I won a packet, but I didn't heed the old boy's advice. I lost it all back and then some. Never gambled since. And stopped shooting grouse to boot." He looked across the lawn. "Well, here are some handsome young ladies come to join us." He held up a tankard of ale, "We'll all toast my daughter Charlotte on her birthday."

A chorus of "Happy Birthday" greeted her as she and her sister and cousin strolled over to the menfolk.

Jack Ellicott came forward to meet them and took Charlotte's hand, offering his congratulations. Then he drew her a little to the side and whispered, "I'd like to see you alone, Char. . . . I have something for you. Let's slip away if we can."

Charlotte reddened slightly. Jack always made her a little uneasy, the way he looked at her. It had been happening steadily for several years. Whenever the families met, he paid her what was to her mind an inordinate amount of attention. It wasn't that she hadn't begun to think about young men, about love and marriage, it was just that . . . well, Jack was her cousin, she had known him as long as she could remember. Nevertheless, she answered, "I'll try." Then she added, "Of course, we're going to cut the cake soon and . . ."

His darkly handsome face grew fierce. "Stop trying to avoid me." Then the scowl softened and he grinned, "I just want to give you a present. . . . It won't take long. And talk to you . . . for a moment. Alone. We never seem to be alone."

She nodded acquiescence. They were now being watched, so she left his side and came to her father who kissed her on the cheek.

"Happy birthday again. . . ." He sighed. "I can't get over it. Seventeen. It seems like yesterday. With Arthur away, I forget that you are all growing up. Even the twins," he said loud enough for all to hear, "seem gigantic. They'll be as tall as you soon. G.H. already is. And he's only twelve."

"Thirteen, father. If he were to hear you, he'd die. I saw him in Arthur's room yesterday, trying on one of Arthur's coats. It was too big for him, but not by much. Yes, it's true your children are growing up."

"I confess, I can hardly accept it. Seventeen is a young lady. Time to think of . . . flying from the nest."

"Are you trying to push me out?" she teased.

"Not at all. But before long some local swain . . . now don't blush. Everyone here is your friend."

"That's why," she said, but that wasn't the whole truth. It was because Jack was standing nearby looking at her again in that funny way.

Aunt Judith called out from the doorway. "Come inside, all of you. It's time to cut the cake. Where is Alfie?"

"Off somewhere with G.H. and Caroline," Ellen called out. "They wouldn't let me come."

"Well, they'll miss their cake if they aren't careful." Judith Ellicott retreated inside and the others began to follow.

Charlotte blew out all the candles with one breath, which meant, of course, that she was going to have good luck the following year. Then she cut the cake and began serving, by which time the dining hall, the largest room in the house, was a cacophony of sound. Most of the men had been sampling the ale or the rum all afternoon and they were in a boisterous mood. The women, too, were happy, for not only was a seventeenth birthday a joyous occasion, but any holiday of any sort offered a chance to see relatives and neighbors that one had not seen for some time.

Then, to add to the noise and confusion, Alfred Ellicott,

G.H., and Caroline all came into the room dripping wet, soaked to the skin and looking somewhat chagrined. It seemed that they had been to the creek and had tried to cross it on the rocks. The three of them were holding hands when one of them (each accused the other) slipped and, of course, all three went into the water, which was now quite high because it had been a late spring in Suffolk.

Everyone laughed a great deal and the three errant children began to laugh too seeing that they were not to be punished for what had happened. While they were being sent off to change, Jack Ellicott sidled up to Charlotte and suggested that now would be a good time for them to slip away from the throng. Reluctantly she agreed to follow him outside and to meet him on the path that led to the barn and stables.

After she had eaten her cake and had finished her tea, she made her way to the door. No one was paying too much attention to her although she did stop twice to receive more congratulations, best wishes, and the like. Jack had been gone for some time when she finally went through the door into the kitchen and spoke to Cook, whose real name was Agnes Morley but who had been called nothing but Cook ever since Charlotte could remember.

She went out the back door and around the house to the path. Everyone else was still inside. Jack was waiting for her by a giant elm, only a few yards from the house. He smiled at her but his eyes flashed a look of impatience.

He said, "This is for you. The first present, that is."

"The first?"

"There are two."

She took the package, neatly wrapped, and opened it. Inside was a velvet box perhaps three by four inches in size. Carefully she lifted the lid and peered into it. There, on the cushion, was a tiny gold locket on a gold chain. The locket was heart-shaped and by squinting she could see two sets of initials: J.E. & C.L.

"Jack, it's beautiful . . . but you shouldn't have. . . ."

"Why not? It's a very special day. I got it in Bury . . . ordered it months ago. Don't you like it?"

"Oh, yes, I do, but it must have been frightfully expensive, and really you shouldn't . . . the initials. . . . What will people think?"

"Well you don't have to show it, unless you want to. I know what I should *like* them to think. But if you're too shy at the moment . . . just wear it under your . . . next to your heart and think of me."

"I don't know that I should accept it . . . and I couldn't keep it a secret. . . . I've never kept secrets. Besides . . ."

"You must know how I feel, Char. Don't worry, I'll wait for you. For a while. But I want you to be . . . thinking of me. I want you . . . not to see others—understand? It's time you were wed. My mother was sixteen when she married.

"But mine was eighteen. . . ."

"All the more reason, then; you're right in between. I want to marry you, Char. That's a proposal, I guess."

"No, I won't. . . . I don't want to think about marriage yet. Not for a while."

"All right. I won't say anything. But I'll be here, be around, and sooner or later . . . you'll have me. Here's your other present."

Swiftly before she was aware of what was happening, he grabbed her in his powerful arms and brought his mouth to hers. It was the first time she had been kissed by a man, the first time another's lips had met hers. She was frightened and she struggled slightly but he held her firm. The sensation was not unpleasant and it was true she had often wondered to herself and sometimes with her cousin, Dunreath, just what it felt like, but at the moment she only knew that she wanted to get away.

Finally he released her. "There, you see, I'm the man for you, Charlotte Linton. That's just a taste of me. You'll see. Before long we'll be wed. Speechless, are you? Go ahead, join the others."

She turned away from him, trying to compose herself, but she suddenly felt a need to get away from him as quickly as possible, so she started to run up the path.

"Happy birthday," he called after her.

CHAPTER TWO

At the time the three older girls trooped into the kitchen to examine the birthday cake, Aunt Judith and Margaret had, as the girls suspected, been engrossed in a deeply private conversation. It did not matter that Cook was there. Cook knew all the family secrets and had never even hinted at one of them. She listened, but seldom spoke, offering advice only if it were sought, and even then only if she was sure the seeker truly wanted to know what she thought.

She was busy kneading dough for the next day's bread while the two sisters-in-law were in deep discussion. Margaret was explaining that they hoped for a good harvest in the fall for the last one had been poor and money was going to be tight for the time being at Linton Park.

"We shan't starve," she said, smiling. "Nothing like that. But we have to pull in the belt, that's the way Henry puts it. Naturally I'm concerned, but mostly about Charlotte. She's of an age now. She doesn't seem to have much inclination to find a beau. I think she doesn't want to grow up. She likes it here. But she should be out in the world, meeting people. She should meet some London folk. The lads in Suffolk are fine boys, but there is a delicacy about Charlotte and I don't think she would be happy living with a farmer. It isn't that we think she's too good for them, but her interests . . . she plays so well, she adores music, and she paints. She's very outgoing and friendly, but . . . we'd like for her to have a good match."

"You'd like for her to meet a man with money of his own, not someone who'll be another burden here."

"Heavens, any man could be a help at Linton Park. But he'd have little to look forward to, for Arthur is to inherit.

The girls will get some money and of course they could always live here, but I don't think it would entice the kind of man who might be right for Charlotte."

"I'm going up to London next week for just a short visit. I'll be back by July. Maybe she could come to me. I could arrange for her to meet a few young men there."

"No, that won't quite do. Charlotte is shy. If she thinks she's on exhibit like a prize cow she'll have none of it. She needs to get away from here, to be on her own for a few months and meet some men in a more natural way."

"Perhaps she could take employment of some sort."

"Yes, but not in a shop. That would never do. But she is good with children and has a number of accomplishments such as music and sewing and of course she was a good student. She knows her sums, even knows some Latin."

"A governess in a nice family . . ."

"That would be ideal, but positions like that are hard to come by, I'm sure."

"Perhaps, but I'll ask about and write to you right away if I hear of anything. Do you think Charlotte would be agreeable?"

"She may not want to go at first, but I think I can convince her. I can always tell her we can use the money, small amount that it will be, and that we would have one less mouth to feed." Margaret chuckled. "Much difference that would make. But it might convince her—just for a few months, that's all."

"I'll see what I can do," Judith responded. "Now I think it is time to cut the cake. . . ."

Later that night, when everyone was in bed, Margaret brought up the subject with her husband. Henry, despite the fact that he was an outgoing person, had never been an easy person for Margaret to talk to when it came to the children. He thought the raising of children was women's work and he was pleased at the way Margaret went about it, so he seldom commented or interfered.

When she had finished talking, he said, "I think Jack's sweet on her."

"That's hardly a good thing."

"Why? He'll be rich one day. Dunreath Manor, all the family money."

"They're first cousins. Oh, I know it's common enough,

but it's not healthy, really. Besides, I don't think she likes him that way. She's nervous when he's about."

"Maybe that's because she's shy."

"No, it's different. He was always a little wild . . . mean, too, as a child. I think she fears him."

"Well, it's too bad. Keep everything in the family. Much prefer him to some London rake . . . or one of the local clods. The lad has spirit, that's all. Marriage would settle him down. Responsibility, babies . . ."

"Not necessarily. No, Jack's a bad'un, I think, and I'd rather she didn't see too much of him."

"Speak, then." her husband said. "Must say it's bound to offend George and Judith."

"I certainly *won't* say anything to Charlotte—nor will you. Send her right into his arms, I should think. We'll just see if we can get her off to London. To visit Judith. And maybe she'll be offered a job. It should seem to happen naturally."

"For an upright woman, you do a lot of conniving."

"That's how I got you."

"I've no doubt. But don't tell me about it. Let me live in bliss, thinking I won the fairest lass in all Suffolk. Don't tell me that she trapped me, that I don't want to know."

"All right, dear Henry, you'll never know. But I'm going to speak to Charlotte in the morning. Tell her as a birthday present she is to spend a few days in London with Judith, say, in a week or so. She will be pleased."

"Conniving. I married a conniving woman."

"Just protecting my chicks a little while longer. Soon enough she'll be on her own. Well, we always taught them to stand on their own two feet. Now we can put it to the test."

"Arthur," her husband reminded her.

"Yes, he went away, but he's not going to make career of it. Five years at most."

"It was his decision, stood on his own two feet, and told me in the library."

"I remember. I hope he's safe. We ought to have a letter from him soon. He might be getting leave. . . ."

"Soon, yes. Don't fret, Marg. He'll be fine. There's not even a war going on."

"But ships, the sea. I don't understand it. We're miles from water. I just don't understand. . . ."

"He needed to get away from us, from the whole family and sow a few wild oats before he settles down. I couldn't afford to send him on a trip to the Continent or set him up in London. This way he travels free and saves a little besides. He's a good lad, don't you worry none about him."

"No. Right now, all my worries are concentrated on Charlotte." She didn't tell her husband one thing, a rarity for her, for she confided fully in Henry Linton on most occasions. She didn't tell him that Charlotte had shown her the locket, recounted the proposal, and then, almost as an afterthought so as to hide her real embarrassment, mentioned the kiss.

No, Charlotte Linton was not going to marry her cousin Jack Ellicott no matter how close the two families were. Not if she didn't wish to marry him. Margaret believed in marrying for love. She had; Judith had. And Charlotte was going to be no different. Charlotte was going to get the man of her choice and that man was obviously not Jack Ellicott, for which Margaret was eternally grateful.

While Margaret and Henry were sleeping, Charlotte and Anne, who shared a room, sat up talking. The night air was balmy although there was a hint of rain in the sky and they had the windows open from which one could, if one got out of bed, crossed the room, and leaned out far enough, see a little sliver of moon. Neither girl at the moment was interested in the moon, though. They were talking about Charlotte's encounter with Jack.

"What was it like?" Anne was asking, "Being kissed?"

"I don't know, it happened so fast. I wasn't expecting it. I was afraid."

"Didn't you just hate it?"

"No. But I didn't relish it, either. I guess I wasn't in the mood or something."

"But doesn't that mean you're engaged? I thought you only kissed a man after you got engaged."

"That's just custom, what polite society says you must do. In the country they don't always go by those rules. Remember Norma." Norma Kean was a local girl who had been forced at the age of fifteen into a rather hasty marriage. She was always used by the older folks as an example to their young girls. Embraces should come after a formal engagement. It wasn't explicitly added, but the message was clear: if something happened after an engagement the marriage date could always be brought forward a few weeks or a month. Living as they did in the country, the Linton girls were not ignorant of certain biological facts; it was only a completely pure innocence that was maintained. From farm life they vaguely understood reproduction, but they had no experience whatsoever and an illicit kiss was probably the most exciting event for both of them, although Charlotte wanted desperately for Anne to believe that it had been unimportant.

"But the locket," she said. "That is different. I don't know whether I should accept it."

"What did Mother say?" asked Anne, for Charlotte had already informed her that she had told their mother everything.

"Oh, you know Mother. She never says much. She said he shouldn't have kissed me, it wasn't a gentlemanly thing to do, and that when he thought it over he would probably apologize. She said maybe I shouldn't be with him too much, but that's hard when they're always here or we're there at the Manor."

"But what did she say about the locket? May I see it again?"

"Here." Charlotte handed over the velvet box. "She said it looked like real gold and must have cost a pretty penny. Mother is always practical first."

"Did she say you have to give it back?"

"I said she was practical, didn't I. I can keep it if I think of it as a birthday token from a cousin and friend. If I start to think it means anything else—or if Jack insists that it does—then I must give it back. Oh, yes, she suggested that I put it away in the box in a drawer for the time being." Charlotte reached and took back the box, closed the lid, and got up from the bed where they were both reclining. "And that is what I am going to do right now."

"Are you going to do that?"

"I just did. I put it away."

"No, what mother said. Stay away from him when he's here. And when we visit Dunreath."

"She didn't exactly say stay away from him. I just should not let him have another opportunity . . . be in groups, she meant."

"Do you think he'll apologize? I doubt it."

13

"So do I. But he should. He will if he is a true gentleman. If Arthur were home, I could tell him and have him thrash Jack."

"That might be difficult. Besides, they're friends."

"Sort of. Not so much any more. Jack got into too many scrapes. I heard father and Arthur talking. That was why Arthur wanted to go to sea, to get away. At least it was one of the reasons."

"You were listening at the keyhole?"

"Pssh. The door was open out into the garden. I was picking flowers. That was all I heard, really."

"No it wasn't, Char. I can tell. What else?"

"Only that Papa said money was tight this year. If it weren't for that he would have lent some to Arthur to take a year abroad."

"So instead he had to join the navy."

"I think he wanted to. . . . He didn't want father's money. And there was another thing. . . ."

"Charlotte! You *were* listening—to the whole conversation."

"Well, not all of it. I couldn't hear it all."

They both laughed and then Anne said, "What else? Come on now, don't tease. What else?"

"Dunreath is in love with Arthur—and he is with her, too, I think—but she's too sickly to marry. So it is better that they be apart."

Ann sighed. Romantic love was her quest. She kept several books hidden among her things, stories of unrequited love, of young love cut off by death. And here in her own family . . . Naturally everyone knew that Dunreath was smitten with Arthur, but it was such a quiet thing— Dunreath was so shy and withdrawing and Arthur hardly ever paid her any mind unless she was sick—oh, it was truly romantic!

"Wouldn't that be funny," she said, "if you married Jack and Arthur married Dunreath. Then Alfie could marry Posie." She fell back on her bed laughing as hard as possible.

"You're being silly. I already told you I'm not interested in Jack—nor in any man. And Arthur is away. And Posie is too young to marry." The idea struck her funny, too, and she fell beside her sister, laughing equally as hard. Finally she stopped and said, "How silly it all is—love."

"I don't think it is silly at all. Look at Mother and Father. Or Aunt Judith and Uncle George."

"Or Norma and the Crowley boy."

Anne, who, despite her romanticism, had a logical streak, said, "How do you know they aren't wildly happy?"

"Perhaps. But I think they were too young. I shan't marry till I'm much, much older and am in danger of becoming an old maid."

"When you're twenty, you mean."

"Oh, you. I meant old. Really old. Twenty-five."

"What will you do until then?"

"Stay here. Teach Posie and Beth and Ellen and G.H. Help Mother and Father. Work in the village . . . church work. Volunteers are always needed. I'd keep busy, I assure you."

"I predict . . ." Anne said.

"Yes . . ."

"I predict you shall marry a London dandy—within the year."

"You are a very poor seer. I shan't even be in London this year. None of us shall."

"Perhaps he'll come here."

"A London dandy. He couldn't stand the smell. And the dirt on his boots. And our country food. And besides, no one here speaks French. How would he communicate?"

"With his kisses, I suppose." More paroxysms of laughter from Anne, until Charlotte finally reached over and pushed her pillow over her sister's face.

Burrowing out from under, Anne added, "A London dandy with a fortune who loves you as much as you love him. So much so that he buys a place nearby just so all your little sisters and brothers can come and visit."

"I told you, I intend to wait."

"Until you fall in love. That might happen at any time."

"Well, we'll see. First I have to get to London and that is not likely to happen. I'm going to sleep." She blew out the candle by her bed.

"We'll see, Char. You didn't expect to get a locket or a kiss today and you got both."

"Go to sleep."

Anne climbed over and blew out her own candle and then settled back into her pillows. "G'night, Char. Charlotte Linton, lovely lady of London."

"Good night, Anne, named after the Regent's wife, whom he shortly thereafter divorced."

"Yes, I was to be the favored one—now it's Caroline."

"If he doesn't divorce again."

"Well, I hope he marries a Charlotte, then. Perhaps you . . ."

"Oh, go to sleep."

But when they slept, it was Charlotte Linton who dreamed of London.

CHAPTER THREE

The two letters arrived by post the same day. Often there were weeks that went by without any communication from the outside world and it was a rare day indeed when two letters arrived at Linton Park. One was from Arthur Linton and it was marked on the outside with some exotic lettering that they all decided was Arabic. The other was from Aunt Judith in London.

Everyone was present, for a letter was always important—and one from the oldest child, away at sea, was bound to contain news and comments for each and every person in the family, for that was Arthur's way. He never forgot anyone. Naturally his was opened first by Margaret Linton, for it was addressed to her, and she was a far better reader than her husband.

She read:

My Dearest Mother and Family,

This is to let you know that I am well and enjoying myself very much in His Majesty's Service. I am writing from Egypt! Can you imagine, the mysterious Nile, crocodiles, brown men with sheets over them, giant pyramids? I have seen it all for we restocked in Port Said and had a short leave, going to Alexandria and then seeing the pyramids and a small sphynx. It is all not beauty of course, for the people are poor, disease-ridden, and garbage of all sorts is everywhere. They are loud, screaming at us most of the time for money, but they mean no harm. I attempted the food only once and got horribly sick, so I think I will only have the coffee which is thick and sweet and doesn't seem to effect me. It is very hot, of course, but there is a breeze at night and a lot of us sleep above decks. So far no one has complained. My mates are all fine fellows as I told you before, from good families and many of them intend to make the Navy their career. Some of them are third and fourth generation, can you imagine that? So far, despite the fact that I am a "land-lubber," I have not been sick at sea, but the weather has not been bad in the Mediterranean. Still, if I survived the trip from Portsmouth to Gibralter, they tell me I can survive everything. I have become good friends with a chap my own age. His name is Edward Delacour and he is from London and his father is some bigwig in the Admiralty, but Edward is very quiet about it. I hope to bring him home with me, which should be in a few months.

"I hope he's handsome," Caroline said, but they all told her to be quiet.

Enough about me. Except to say I like the Navy, but I miss Linton Park, especially as I know it is spring. Now, how are all of you? I hope, Mother, that you are getting enough rest and that the girls are helping the way they should. And that G.H. is not being too much of a pest. Tell him I shall bring him a regular Ensign's cap, insignia and all, if he promises to behave.

Happy birthday, Charlotte. I know this letter will be late by several weeks but tomorrow is your birthday. I have bought you a present but I shall bring it home with me as it is quite small and I don't want to trust it to the post. Now that you are seventeen, you will be looking for a beau. Make sure you take your time. I would like you to meet my friend, Edward.

Caroline made a mock wailing sound, but they ignored her.

I am sure you will like him, and he you.

Father, have you enough help for the August harvest? I was thinking that my first leave will come about then and you can count on my two willing hands as soon as I get home. The Kean boys should be old enough to do a full day's work now and I am sure there are plenty more in the district who are needy. I hope everything is growing fast and that you have had enough rain. Have you done any hunting? The one thing I miss—that and riding. I took a camel ride but it just wasn't the same!

How are you, Anne? Anxious to become seventeen, too? In less than a year . . . it is hard to believe how old we have gotten. I remember the year you fell out of the tree and I carried you up to the house. You must have been seven or eight and I was a lot more scared than you were. You are easily the bravest of us all. I'm not brave at all. I still have nightmares about being lost at sea. And when they shoot a cannon, just in drill or for ceremony, I hold my ears.

Tell Caroline that the women all go around with their heads covered and there are no tomboys, so I don't think she'd like it here. You can hardly fish, Car and G.H., because of the crocodiles. They're very fast and they have a lot of mean-looking teeth. When they come up on the banks to sun, we all scatter, but the natives just laugh. Occasionally the natives catch one and eat it but I think it is illegal. I don't know whether they boil it in a pot (it would have to be a big pot) or roast it. I don't intend to try any.

Ellen should know, since she will be studying history this year, that Egypt is a civilization much older than ours. They seem backward now, but they just stopped growing a thousand years ago when we started. But they gave us paper and symbols for numbers and letters and the ways to make wells and irrigate unfertile land. In other words, learn from them, Ellen, don't just think of them as a lot of heathenish natives (which they are at the moment). Someday they may be great again.

Now, to the twins. Stay out of mischief. Help your mother. If you're good girls, I may have a little surprise for you when I get home, something no other girl in Suffolk will have.

I miss you all more than I can say—and send all of my love to you. You are in my prayers every night, as is Dunreath. By the way, I hope she is well. I have written her a separate letter in case she is not at Linton Park when this arrives. Pray for me.

> Your affectionate and obd.
> son and brother,
>
> Arthur Linton

They were all excited by the contents of the letter and especially by the fact that Arthur was half-way around the world in a strange and exotic place seeing things that all of them had heard of but none imagined he or she would ever see.

"He seems in good spirits," Henry said.

"Yes, Father, he does," Anne replied. "I think he likes the traveling, but I'm not sure he likes the Navy."

"He's made friends," Caroline said. "A good friend. Look out, Charlotte."

"I don't want to marry a man who is away all the time. You can have him, Car."

"Caroline's too young for him," Ellen said.

"I won't be too young for long. By the time he gets here I'll be almost fifteen. Besides, when he sees how beautiful and brilliant I am, he'll agree to wait a year or two. He can go off to sea and think about me. That's exactly the kind of man I want, Char, one who isn't always around."

Henry Linton said, "Like your father?"

"Oh, daddy. You're different. Besides you sometimes go away."

"Well, I always want him here," his wife replied. "That's where we differ, Caroline."

"Edward Delacour. What a romantic name. Of the heart. I just hope he waits for me. Char doesn't want him. . . . I suppose Anne . . ."

"You can have him, love. I don't want a seafarer, either."

Margaret interrupted the banter. "Well, since all of this is unlikely to ever happen—and it is a great possibility that Mr. Delacour will find none of you suitable, especially if your manners are as they have been this morning—perhaps I should read Aunt Judith's letter now."

There was a chorus of "do" and they all settled back while Margaret unsealed the missive.

It was far shorter than Arthur's, for not only had Aunt Judith been away from Suffolk but a short time but it was not in her nature to write lengthy letters. They were always succinct and usually had a point that she wished to make, as was the case with this one, although the point was not at once obvious.

Dear Margaret and Henry and all the children:

London is lovely but we have had quite a bit of rain. I hope some of it has gone north. If nothing else it cleans the streets, for it seems that each time I return the city is somehow dirtier. It makes one almost wish never to go abroad. However, I have had numerous invitations (the price one pays for staying away so long) and have therefore been out a considerable amount and of course I have had my own "at homes" twice a week, so all in all I have been busy. George joins me next week (he swears) and that will make things a little easier.

I saw your sister, Henry, Lady Fitzhugh and little Cedric (why is he called that? He is thirty and rather roly-poly, a bit of a pudding) and they send their regards and hope to see you and Margaret soon. Lady Fitzhugh had me to tea and introduced me to a charming woman, a Mrs. Forbes who has just taken a house by St. James Park, on Prospect Lane, near Lady Chamberley's. A most desirable address. Her husband, James, has been given the garter for some service or other and she is rather full of herself but seems a good-hearted person, though a bit vague. They have two young children around the ages of the twins and Ellen I should gather, a boy and a girl. The reason for this long preamble about people you do not know is that Mrs. Forbes is most anxious to find a suitable governess for her children. She has had three in two years and they have all proved unsuitable (who was at fault I will not pretend to understand) but she has indicated that they were of somewhat advanced years and she is now ready to try a younger lady, one with experience with young children and with some accomplishments, such as music, and can teach reading and sums, yet comes from a good family.

It occurred to me that Charlotte might be interested

in such a position for a few months or longer. She seems to be the ideal person, and when I mentioned her, Lady Fitzhugh spoke highly of her. Mrs. Forbes seemed most taken with the idea and asked if it would be possible to see Charlotte at once. I told her Charlotte was in Suffolk but that I would write and ask her to come to visit me for a short stay and at that time she and Mrs. Forbes could become acquainted.

Naturally, if Charlotte is not interested, you need only apprise me of that fact. And, of course, if she comes and then does not take to Mrs. Forbes or the children, she would be under no obligation. By the same token, Mrs. Forbes would not be obligated should she find Charlotte unsuitable, a fact I doubt will be the case for she seems desperate and Charlotte could hardly be unsuitable to anyone.

Well, I have already written a longer letter than usual. Talk this over and send me a note letting me know what you decide to do. I should hope you will not procrastinate, and I think it might be an interesting opportunity for you, Charlotte, a change of scenery where you will meet some new people. It need not last for a long time. I close with all my love to all of you,

As ever,

Judith Dunreath Ellicott

All at once the room was abuzz with talking; it seemed that everyone had something to say at once. Charlotte going to London! Their own Charlotte! A chance to meet . . . What were the children like? . . . Where was Prospect Lane? . . . Friends of Lady Fitzhugh, their other aunt, don't you remember Cedric, the pudding? Charlotte is in luck, so lucky. . . . We'll miss her. . . . What a glorious prospect . . . yes, Prospect Lane. Of course you may come home, you goose—and often . . . with a beau, perhaps. Maybe she doesn't want to go. How could anyone not want?

Charlotte fled from the room.

Her father found her later, standing by the pond, the one he and his father had made by damming up the stream for the cattle. Now, though, the cattle were in the fields and his oldest daughter, Charlotte, was standing below the barn, staring into the pond as if trying to read her future from the barely moving water.

"Well, daughter, what a lot of hub-bub. You'd think you'd been asked to join Arthur in Egypt and teach the little ones of the Khedive. You don't want to go, is that it? You don't have to, you know? Judy was just putting a proposition, something she thought might be good for you—to get away from Linton Park for a while."

"No, I *want* to go. It isn't that."

"You want to go? Well, I'll be.... They're all up at the house with long faces saying what's the matter with Charlotte, it's a wonderful opportunity. You want to go for sure?"

"Yes, of course. It *is* a wonderful opportunity. I've always been at home and I'll miss you all and I know you'll miss me, but you said on my birthday I have to try my wings, fly from the nest a little. It's not forever, after all, only a few months, a chance to meet new people with different ways...."

"Are you afraid of the London folk?"

"No. Aunt Judith lives there and she's wonderful."

"They won't all be like Aunt Judith."

"Oh, I know that. But I'm not really afraid. It's just all so new. Sort of the end of something . . . being a child here at Linton Park. Now I'll be a grown-up. Oh, Anne would go in a minute. So would Caroline. They're different. But I'll go. I want to go. I need to get away—and there's another good thing, too. I'll be earning wages and I can send some home the way Arthur does . . . to tide you over."

"Yes you will. Until the crops come in. Let me do it. I want to. It will make me feel like an adult."

"But there will be things in London you'll want...."

"I have plenty of good things, Papa. And I can sew. I shan't be going to fancy parties or balls, after all. I shall be fine just as I am."

"Well, that's very thoughtful of you, Char. It'll be put to good use. The way things look, this year's gonna be a rare harvest, but last year wasn't so good, as you know...."

"I know. I want to help." She took his hand, added teasingly, "Besides with me away, that's like having two less mouths to feed."

"Don't try to gammon me, young lady. The twins each eat more than you and they're half your age. If I wanted to save at table, I'd send those two packing."

She laughed and he joined her. "Well, I'll look around and see if there's work for a couple of imps who eat too much."

"Include G.H. if you can. Oh, there's work for imps in London. Satan's imps, which thank God, mine aren't. Just devilish enough to try their mother, they are."

"And me sometimes."

"Yes, they'll miss you most, those twins."

"You know who I'll miss most, besides you and Mother?"

"Who?"

"Dunreath."

"Poor young'un. Well, maybe she'll come to visit you."

"She's bound to. If she's feeling up to the trip."

"And Jack with her."

There was no answer, and for a moment both were lost in their own reflections.

Conniving women, his wife and sister-in-law, Henry thought. Getting her away from Linton Park, getting her away from the country. Getting her away from Jack Ellicott, that was their main reason. There was more he didn't know, of that he was sure. But with women, there was always more you didn't know and would probably never find out.

"Come on up to the house," he said, "there's plans have to be made. We'll all miss you, Char, but it seems a fine opportunity. And I'm sure you know what you're doing."

"Oh, Papa . . ." She put her arms around his neck. "I love you so. I love all of you. I'll miss you. But I'll be back. I promise."

CHAPTER FOUR

Turmoil reigned for a brief time at Linton, much as it had when Arthur Linton was about to set off to sea. From the dusty attic a huge trunk was carried down, cleaned, the fittings oiled. In Charlotte's room clothes were separated, studied, discarded, repaired, washed, ironed, and in some cases passed down to Anne (who was about Charlotte's size) but usually to Caroline who was a little smaller still, although she promised from the look of her to grow up to be the largest of the Linton girls.

Charlotte was to leave within the week. Leave for London! Before going, however, she had to see Dunreath and so she set off accompanied by Anne only (to the acute dismay of the other children) on the half-a-days' journey to Dunreath Manor. They were driven in the small carriage, although, they swore they could drive themselves, by William Clapp, a one-legged ex-soldier who was an expert with horses and who had lived in and run the stable for twenty-eight years when coming back from the war with the colonies, he applied to Henry Linton for a job, refusing outright a pension. His family had been in Suffolk as long as the Lintons, longer he claimed, and he would not be put out to pasture. He wanted an honest job and he'd show the squire he could do an honest day's work. He got the job, did more than a day's work every day, never complained, and taught every Linton how to ride a horse by the time he or she was five. He had taught the Ellicott children as well.

So he drove them over the rough and somewhat muddy road to Dunreath Manor singing, as he always did, a raucous song learned in the service, one which all of the family tactfully ignored.

"Maybe Dunreath will come to visit with you," Anne said.

"I hope so. I was going to write and ask her but then it occurred to me that since she didn't accompany Aunt Judith she may not be well enough to travel. Perhaps she'll come up later. I hope so."

"She'll want to be home when Arthur gets his leave."

"Yes, except he'll come to London first. Oh, I wish," Charlotte added, "she would get fully well. Do you think they'll ever marry?"

"I hope so. It would make her so happy. Perhaps when Arthur is through with the Navy. He'll be twenty-six then and she'll be twenty-two. By then she may be better. The doctors say there is nothing they can do. They say pray."

"And we do. I mention Dunreath in my prayers every night, Anne."

"So do I."

"That's the trouble with having so large a family and so many relatives. Your prayers take so long."

"Yes, but by the time you are finished you're almost asleep. It's better than counting sheep."

By midafternoon they could see the outlines of Dunreath Manor, a house not much larger than their own but far grander. They turned into a circular gravel drive that led them to the front steps. The noise of the horse and carriage was loud enough that by the time they reached their destination several servants were standing on the top steps ready to greet them. And Dunreath, from a second floor window, called down to say how glad she was that they had come and that she would be down momentarily. They had no more than disembarked and had their overnight valise handed down when Dunreath, followed by Alfie, came flying from the door. As soon as he saw that it was only the two older girls, Alfie sulked away, disappointed, for he had hoped that G.H. might have accompanied them.

"I was expecting you," Dunreath said. "I got a letter from Mother telling me about your wonderful offer and I knew you wouldn't go to London, Char, without seeing me. I would have come to you myself, but I have been rather tired since the day of your birthday. Have you heard from Arthur? I received a letter from him just the day before yesterday. From Egypt. He seems very well and happy." Dunreath's color was high, in fact she seemed a bit flushed and her speech was more rapid than usual.

The three young ladies embraced and then went inside the house where tea was ordered sent to Dunreath's room, a large, comfortable room, sunny with matching yellow spread and curtains, a room designed to keep the occupant cheerful.

They were chatting amiably when tea arrived. Dunreath poured and Charlotte could not help noticing that her hand shook ever so slightly when she passed the cups.

"So, Char, you are off to London."

"How do you know that I have accepted? I almost didn't, you know."

"Oh, I was sure you would. It seems such a wonderful opportunity. I know you'll miss everyone—and we'll miss you—but when I got Mama's letter and she said she had written to Aunt Margaret, I was sure in my heart that you would take the opportunity. Sometimes I have a kind of second sight. I know that certain things are going to happen. I shall miss you."

"But surely you'll be coming to London?"

"I don't know. Right now, I am very tired. I sleep all the time. Then for a time I am better. Today I was restless. I sensed you were coming. I wasn't surprised at all. In a few days, when Papa goes up, I may accompany him. Jack and Alfie will go for certain and that would leave me all alone here, except the servants, of course."

Anne said, "You can come stay with us. Sleep with me. Since Char won't be there."

"That's very kind. No, I imagine I'll be well enough to go. I hope. Then, too, Arthur will be home soon. Perhaps we'll meet in London . . . but enough about me. Let's talk about Charlotte going off on a great adventure. Aren't you excited, Charlotte? Doesn't it at all intrigue you, London and the Forbes family and Prospect Lane and a whole different way of life, if only for a few months."

"In a way. I guess I'm not the adventurer of the family. Arthur and Caroline, I think, are the ones who yearn for far-off places. Me, I should be content in Suffolk, in Linton Park forever. But I'm sure it will be an education— and a worthwhile experience."

"Oh don't sound so superior," Anne laughed. "You'll love it—and meet many fine gentlemen, too. That's adventure of the right sort. More than you'd meet in Linton Park."

"Jack was angry, I know, when he heard about it," said Dunreath. "He, at least, doesn't want you to leave. I told him his best chance with you was to let you find your own way—but no one has ever been able to counsel Jack, least of all his sister."

Charlotte rose and went to the window. Across the lawn she could see the large pond and the swans moving gracefully to and fro. Clumps of trees dotted the undulating hills, making dark shadows on the verdant grass. The rose-red brick house with the gray-white roof was not unlike their own but it was was far more sedate. There seemed to be less bustle at Dunreath Manor, as though no one there really did any work, a fact she knew not to be true. It was so peaceful here, and she supposed were she to marry Jack, some day it would be hers. Quickly she turned away. It was not what she wanted. He was not what she wanted. She did not want to hurt Dunreath, for Jack was her brother, but she would never be able to marry him.

"A copper for your thoughts?" Anne asked.

"How lovely this view is, Dunreath. I am sorry that Jack is unhappy. But there are many reasons why I must go and take this position."

Dunreath, who really was the kindest of persons, said, "Darling Charlotte, I understand, believe me, I do. It will all be for the best. It is time someone curbed Jack a little bit, anyway. He has always been too sure of himself. Not that he's a bad person . . . but a little thoughtless sometimes. It will do him good to cool his heels for a time. Until you know your own mind."

And then, Charlotte thought, if I feel as I do now, that my life does not have room for him, how will he take it? Well, perhaps by then he will find another.

She turned to them and said, "Did Aunt Judith say much about the Forbes family to you? She mentioned that she met them with Lady Fitzhugh and that Mrs. Forbes seemed a nice enough person. They must have enormous wealth to have a home by St. James Park."

"Yes, he is in shipping, I believe, and was just knighted.

According to Mother they seem quite nice but a little lost in the society of London. Evidently Lady Fitzhugh has taken to them."

Charlotte and Anne looked at one another wide-eyed. Lady Fitzhugh was also their aunt, their father's older sister, and she was perceived by all of the family to be a terrible snob. Although she had been perfectly correct on the few occasions they had encountered her, the rumor was that she disapproved of Henry Linton's marriage to Margaret Ellicott, though no one could understand why. Lady Fitzhugh's husband had died many years ago, leaving her with but one offspring, Fitzhugh Fitzhugh who was called Cedric, a jolly young man of about thirty who was totally unlike his mother. He was not considered bright, but was extremely good-hearted. So far he had never contemplated marriage, much to his mother's dismay.

But for Lady Fitzhugh to have become friends with a newcomer, a person just entering into London society, that was quite a surprise.

However, being a friend of Lady Fitzhugh was as good a passport into London society as one could have, so there was no doubt about the Forbes's credentials. The three girls agreed that Charlotte would enjoy her stay with them and would no doubt be of help to the youngsters.

"And you will like London, Charlotte, I know you will. Once you get over your fear there are so many carriages, so much noise—but at heart the people are good. They have different ways than we have here in the country—oh, but mother will be there with you to help and advise you. And you'll meet all sorts of interesting people. Poets and musicians and painters. And great men in government and finance. It will be an active life compared to Linton Park. How I envy you. To be able to be active all of the time, while I must husband my strength." She stopped and blushed. "I mean I must not try to do too much."

They all laughed. It was not surprising that the word "husband" was on all their minds, despite their protestations to the contrary.

"But tell me, coz, what should I see in London? I have been there so seldom and then only to shop. But there must be many sights, places of historical interest to take the children."

"Westminster Abbey, of course, for you will almost certainly go to church there. At least you should once. And there are museums, and the House of Lords and the House of Commons and many old buildings and bridges. Then, there's the Tower of London, that might frighten them some for it did me. And there are plays to see but not for children, I should imagine, not for ladies, either, from what I am told. But still, all attend the plays and the concerts and some even go to the opera but 'tis much screeching and waving of arms."

"And if I wish just to walk . . . ?"

"You will be a stone's throw from St. James' Park and then there's the palace on the other side and little places by the Thames where book sellers have their stalls and of course there are the shops which can entertain you a whole day just looking at the fashions new from France that everyone laughs at and then goes out and purchases and you see the same ladies who laughed one day wearing the garment the next."

"It sounds a silly place," Anne said.

"All cities are silly places, compared to country life. But they have many good things to recommend them, too. The people are lively and ideas are exchanged. Yes, I like the city," Dunreath said, "and so will Charlotte, no matter how much she protests. And the best part is, you can—"

"Yes?" The two sisters chorused.

"You can always come back to Suffolk. Pity those poor souls who have nothing but the city. We have the best of both worlds and are very fortunate. And, before I forget, it is not unusual while you are abroad to come across the Regent. He seems to be everywhere. Just curtsy and don't speak unless he speaks to you. Then answer his questions. He has a reputation of a rake but he would never approach a decent woman that way."

"My," Charlotte said, "for someone who has been such a recluse, Dunreath, you know a great deal about the city."

"Mama writes me everything, and when she is here she tells me all about her adventures, all the gossip, for she knows I weary of being about the house so much. Sometimes I feel that I can never read another book. How I wish I could ride, ride far away from here, across the hills, into the mountains, free and well, with never a care in my heart." She stopped and looked around embarrassed. "You must think me cracked in my head. How I do go on!" After a moment's silence, she added, "I shall miss you so, Char. But I promise to come to London as soon as I am well enough and we shall see all the sights, do everything, and have thousands of beaux to tease and torment. But not too much, for we do not want to hurt their feelings."

It was clear that Dunreath was trying to act in the best of spirits for her cousins even though she was feeling frail. After they had chatted for some time more and had finished the tea and scones, it was Charlotte who suggested that she and Anne would like to rest after their arduous journey. Dunreath quickly complied, no doubt relieved of the duty of playing hostess in her mother's absence.

A servant showed the two Linton girls to the room they always shared when they came to visit, just a few yards down the corridor from Dunreath's own. They agreed that they would meet later for supper when George Ellicott and his son Jack would be back.

When they were alone Charlotte voiced concern over Dunreath, but Anne, the practical one, reminded her older sister that Dunreath had often gone through these "spells" and in a few days she would be well again. Nevertheless, when they went down to a rather informal dinner, Dunreath was not present, having sent her excuses. So Anne and Charlotte ate with their Uncle George and their two cousins, Jack and Alfie.

Uncle George was as good a raconteur as their own father and he kept them all amused with tales of London which he detested, mimicking rather well the manners and affectations of the people he found there. Jack, although he continued to stare at Charlotte, was subdued and polite, as though in front of his father he felt it necessary to be on his best behavior. If he thought her going to London had anything to do with him, he did not show it, but rather encouraged her, teasing his father about the old man's prejudices against what Jack called a "civil" life.

Still, when the meal was over and it was time to retire (for they ate after sundown in Suffolk), he contrived to be alone with Charlotte at the far end of the drawing room as they all were bidding their adieus.

"I shall see you in London. We're all going in two weeks," he said.

"Even Dunreath?"

"She'll be fine by then. She's just having an attack. Mooning over Arthur, if you ask me. Well, I can understand that. I'm looking forward to spending some time with you in London, Char."

"Well, if I take the position, I shall be very busy. And, if I don't, then I imagine I'll come back to Suffolk almost at once."

"You could always stay with us. Mother adores you. We all do."

"I couldn't impose. Besides, I am going to London specifically because of this position and I intend to take it unless they find me unsuitable."

"Now, who could do that?"

"I might not have the right qualifications."

"Bother! They wouldn't know. I've met Rawley Forbes and his sister."

"The children?"

"No, they're cousins. She's rather dumb, but pleasant enough. He's very stern. You know what I mean. Goes to church on Sunday."

"So do I. And so do you, most of the time."

"Not the same. He means it. He doesn't quite approve of London society, yet he wants to be part of it. Now that his aunt has made her move . . . At any rate, they'll be pleased to have you, a niece of Lady Fitzhugh."

"Well, I hope you're right. I want this position. I need it."

"Right. Well, we'll see you in London, then. I'll show you some of the sights. Introduce you to the right people. You'll like it, I'm sure."

"Yes, I'm looking forward to it."

She noticed the others had gone up, but she suspected Anne was at the top of the stairs listening.

"Well, good-night, Jack."

"Good-night, Char. Look, I'm sorry about the other afternoon. I shouldn't have presumed. It was just that it was your birthday. Are we still friends?"

"Of course."

"And you'll think about me and my offer?"

"Of course. But I want to . . ."

"I understand." He took her hand, bent down and kissed

it. "Perfectly proper. You'll see. I can be anything you want. But just remember that I'll always consider you mine. Good-night."

He released her hand and she turned and walked slowly up the stairs, aware that his eyes followed her until she turned the corner and was out of sight.

CHAPTER FIVE

The trip to London was, for Charlotte, uneventful, with two minor and one major exception. It was the first time she had made the trip by public coach and alone and thus there was an air of excitement to her journey. It rained all the way, making the coach several hours late. And Aunt Judith was not there to meet her when finally, exhausted and mud-splattered, the coach and four pulled into the London hostelry where trips north began and ended.

She was not exactly surprised by the fact that she was not met. It was obviously impossible to tell how late the coach would arrive and no doubt Aunt Judith had other, more important things to do. She had hoped, however, that there would be a message from her, a servant perhaps who would help her proceed with her huge trunk and overnight valise to Curzon Street in Mayfair.

Always resourceful, Charlotte set about hiring a hackney but, because of the inclement weather, she was informed that she might have to wait for some time. She was tired and the news depressed her. The dampness had ruined her hair, she felt sticky all over, was in need of a bath and a change of linen, and, in short, was quite uncomfortable—but it seemed there was nothing for it but to wait and hope that some sort of transportation, either from Ellicott House or of the public kind, showed up soon.

She didn't want to go into the tavern but the roof over the porch was not providing much protection from the elements, for the rain was pelting down. At last, when she was about to throw pride to the winds, a gentleman stepped out from the public rooms under the portico to survey the weather.

When he saw her standing there, he bowed, and announced, "Rotten weather, what?"

"No, it is not very pleasant."

"Can't see the need for it. Rain. What good does it do? Might as well be in the tropics."

"Well, I suppose the farmer is grateful."

"Let him be. Keep it around the farms, not in the city. I'm late for an appointment. Knew I shouldn't have stopped round. Had a chum due on the stage. It's going to be days late, I'm told. Thought I'd be able to hire a hack so I let mine go, worse luck. You waiting for the stage?"

"No, for a hackney, too. I just arrived."

"Well, here comes one. Excuse me, I'm off to grab him before someone else . . ."

With that, despite his fine clothes, he dashed down into the yard and leaped into the opening door of the hackney almost knocking over a man stepping out. They had a few words, then the man paid the driver, was handed his valise and tramped into the public room. The driver climbed back onto the seat of the cab and asked the young gentleman where he wished to go. Through it all Charlotte stood watching, annoyed that the young man had usurped her coach, for she had been standing there waiting when he came out. He had not even offered to share the ride with her, although she supposed she would have had to demur— no, she would not have. He was dressed as a gentleman and no doubt would behave like one. And she wanted to get to Aunt Judith's. So much for London gentlemen, she thought.

Once more she was about to forget her pride and step inside the public rooms when she heard through the rain the clatter of horses hooves and carriage wheels on the cobble stones. This time, to her relief, there was a familiar face peering out of the cab window, albeit one that she hardly expected, her cousin Cedric, that is, Fitzhugh Fitzhugh, Lady Fitzhugh's son. From the way he was waving to her it was obvious that he had been sent round to get her, and when she was safely inside and he had seen to it that her trunk was stored up above and her valise by her feet, had climbed back in himself, and given her his big, pudding-like grin, he explained.

That is, he tried to explain, for along with all of his other rather ridiculous attributes, poor Cedric stuttered. He was the most good-hearted of souls and no one ever laughed at him or if they did he took it in good part, but it was like pulling teeth to get a straight, clear sentence out of him.

"I . . . I came . . . in . . . in . . . instead of . . . M, m, m, Missus Elli . . . Ellicott. She was detained." He breathed a sigh of relief, having gotten out a whole sentence finally.

"I imagined so. It was good of you Cedric. How have you been?"

"Jolly, f, f, fine, as always. You . . . you . . . you see . . . she had to . . . to . . . to . . . go out. The stage was . . . late."

"I understand. And she asked you to look round and you did. Don't worry. Your timing was almost perfect. I'd only been waiting a minute."

"Know. Saw it . . . saw it . . . saw it . . . go . . . by." He took a deep breath. When he relaxed his stutter was far less perceptible. "Was in White's. My club. Lunching. Had to miss dessert." He patted his stomach. "It won't . . . miss . . . miss . . . me. Much." He laughed and she joined in. He was really the most good-natured of souls and it was a relief to see him after that rather impudent and rude young man who had practically stolen her hackney.

"Will . . . will you be stay . . . staying long?" Cedric asked.

"I believe so. I am perhaps going to take a position with the Forbes family. Do you know them?"

"Oh, yes, indeed. Mother . . . Mother knows them. I think they want to match me with . . . Miss Forbes . . . but she won't have me, I should ima . . . ima . . . imagine."

"She is a cousin? Of Mrs. Forbes."

"That's right. Very nice girl. Too good for me."

"I'm sure she's not, Ceddy. No one could be too good for you." And in that Charlotte was not dissembling for despite his affliction, Cedric would make any decent woman a fine husband. It had been known for some time by all the Lintons that their Aunt, Lady Fitzhugh, sought a suitable match for her son. The trouble was that she would not have most of the available young women and the few that she would have did not see Cedric's good qualities, but only his rather foolish demeanor and speech. And so, at thirty, Cedric was still a bachelor.

"Nevertheless, I don't think it's in the cards for me to marry. If it were, I should have been over it by now. Of course, it pleases Mother and I don't . . ." Suddenly he realized he was not stuttering and he stopped. "I say, Char . . . you . . . you are a good influence on me. Enough about me. What are you doing going to work for Mrs. Forbes? I didn't know . . . Mother . . . Mother nev . . . never tells . . . tells me . . . anything."

"I shall tell you then, tell you all, but you must swear to keep it a secret."

"Of course. There are things . . . things I don't tell Mother, too." They both laughed.

She recounted as simply as she could her seventeenth birthday party. She told him that the family fortunes although hardly precarious, were at a low ebb and that any financial contribution she might make would be most welcome at home; and she recounted how she felt that a change would be good for her, that she spent too much time with her own family. She didn't specifically mention Jack Ellicott, for that was too embarrassing, but Cedric was not only a good listener, he was a perceptive one. He instinctively understood that there was a situation at Linton Park that made her uncomfortable and that she didn't want to talk about it, at least not directly. And so he did not press her, but merely told her how glad they all were that she would be in London for a while, that his mother would certainly want to see her eldest niece, that the Forbes family were good people but that he did not know the children well, and that if she ever needed anything, anything at all, money or advice or help, she was to come directly to him.

Of course, given his stutter, it took them the balance of the ride to the Ellicott house in Mayfair before he had concluded.

It was still pouring when they got out and a servant girl held an umbrella for them. Much good that will do, Charlotte thought, for I am soaked already. And so is poor Cedric. Fortunately Aunt Judith had just returned and tea was ordered while she sent Charlotte to her room to change into some dry clothes and put Cedric in front of a cozy fire to dry as best he could his coat, trousers, and boots.

Some twenty minutes later when Charlotte Linton returned, in a fresh and dry frock, her hair brushed and feeling altogether better, she found in addition to Aunt Judith and Cedric another person present. It was then that she was introduced to Miss Angelique Forbes, a pert, lively young lady with a roundish face framed by ringlets of brown all about her head. This was the young woman that Lady Fitzhugh had chosen for her son, Charlotte remembered, and she was a connection, some sort of cousin to the Mrs. Forbes with whom Charlotte was seeking a position.

When they were introduced the young woman greeted Charlotte effusively and told her how much she had heard about her. She then apologized for intruding but it seemed that she had an appointment to meet her brother nearby and he did not appear. She was fortunate that she had been able to find a cab who was to take her home but on the way the cab had slipped a wheel in the mud just off Curzon Street where she knew Mrs. Ellicott resided, and so she had presumed to ask asylum until she could find a way to contact her brother and be taken home. Her own home on Prospect Lane was only a few roads away but under the circumstances, until the torrential downpour abated, she had been asked to stay and have tea, which she hoped was not an inconvenience—and Cedric had kindly offered to take her home but that would not be necessary she hoped.

All this was told in a tiny voice that Charlotte was hard pressed to hear for she was used to country voices which were loud and strong, used as they were for hunting and riding as well as drawing room conversations.

Cedric assured Miss Forbes that he would be delighted to escort her but Aunt Judith, before the conversation went on for too long, pointed out that the rain had not abated and that the best and simplest thing was for all to have their tea and a pleasant conversation.

Cedric was not at his best in social situations; his stutter became more pronounced and so he sat as silently as he could, allowing the three ladies to converse among themselves, nodding agreement when it was required but offering little. It was just as well for the talk soon turned to society gossip and Cedric, despite his position as the son of one of its most prominent members, knew little of society and cared even less for it.

Miss Forbes was speaking. "Since you and Lady Fitzhugh are connected, Miss Linton, I am sure you will be seen much in society."

"I don't believe so. I am here, after all, to fulfill a position, but surely you have been told."

"I don't believe so. I believe I heard your name from my cousin's wife, who is now Lady Forbes. My cousin is considerably older than my brother and myself, but I believe I digress. I was saying I heard your name in connection with something, that you were coming to visit Mrs. Ellicott who has been so kind to us. . . . What sort of a position?"

Aunt Judith interrupted. "Lady Forbes is in need of a governess for her two children. She wanted someone young and responsible who would know how to bring them up properly. Charlotte wanted to come to London for a while. She has lived so long at Linton Park in Suffolk and it was thought a change of atmosphere would be beneficial. It seemed a good way to satisfy the needs of your cousins and to afford Charlotte an opportunity to spend some time in London." Her eyes twinkled slightly as she added, "Lady Fitzhugh, Ceddy's mother, concurred heartily."

"What an interesting thing to do. And to think Valerie did not apprise me, how strange. Well, I suppose we won't see so much of you during the season but no doubt at home you will be present. And we will do our best to introduce you. . . ." Miss Forbes's attitude had cooled somewhat. She seemed a bit at a loss for words.

Charlotte said, "I came here really to work with the children. I have six younger than me at home and am used to teaching them. I hope I can be of service. But I don't plan to consider myself part of society, I shan't have the time."

"Not that you won't be most welcome, my dear," Aunt Judith said, "Eh, Ceddy?"

"What's that? Oh, of co . . . co . . . course. Jo . . . jolly welcome. Anywhere."

"You shall certainly be invited here, Charlotte, and I know there will be other invitations, but you will have to explain that you are simply not free. People will understand. The right people will, at any rate."

"Tell me," Charlotte said, to change the subject and also because she was genuinely curious, "Miss Forbes, what are the children like?"

"Well, Lisette is nine. We seem to go in for rather extraordinary names in our famiy. She is nine and very pretty, but rather sassy. She's rather picked on by her brother, James, James Junior actually, and he's called Juny which he hates, by his mother and so Lisette calls him that, too. He needs the company of other boys, I think, next year he shall go to public school. Harrow, I believe. In the meantime he gets into all sorts of mischief. I confess to trepidations when they are around and we are entertaining. But then I am not overly fond of children. My brother detests them I think."

"I'm sure they have many fine qualities."

"Oh, they do, Miss Linton. Their mother will tell you that. She sees them as paragons. But I suspect you will have your hands full. But we must not have you pessimistic before the fact. The house on Prospect Lane is lovely. Do you know the Lane? Just by St. James Park?"

"No, I am afraid I don't."

"It is next door to Lady Chamberley, a most distinguished woman. Her daughter, you know, eloped. It was quite a scandal. But all is right now. It seems he was a man of good character, an army officer. They are living with his family, somewhere in the north, no doubt in your area. He is quite well-to-do and, of course, Lucy will be rich some day, providing her mother forgives her. But what was I saying? The house . . . overlooking the park. It is quite large. My brother and I live there with them. We are orphans, so to speak. Our parents are no more. So we have been taken in by James and Valerie. We have money of our own, but as I am alone in the world it would not be seemly for me to live alone, and therefore it is practical for my brother to stay there, too. You shall find us a congenial family. We don't see much of the children. But there is oodles of room. You will like it. But I have talked on and on and have given you no opportunity to speak. I do beg your forgiveness, Miss Linton."

"I really have little to say. London is so new to me. I am looking forward to meeting Lady Forbes and Sir James and the children."

"And my brother. You will like Rawley. He's very much a London gentleman."

At that point they were interrupted by the butler who

said that a Mr. Rawley Forbes was at the door and that he was in hopes that his sister might be present. Aunt Judith told him to send the young man in.

He came bustling through the door, all apologies. "I do beg your pardon, Mrs. Ellicott. This has been a terrible day. I was to meet my sister and could not find transportation and consequently I was late. I went home but she was not there, either. I went out again and came across a hackney with a thrown wheel and from the description given me by the driver I deduced that my sister may have sought refuge here. Oh, I beg your pardon."

Mrs. Ellicott said, "I believe you know Cedric Fitzhugh." The two men bowed. "And this is my niece from Suffolk, who will be living I believe with your family, as governess to the children, Miss Charlotte Linton. Mr. Rawley Forbes."

It was obvious that he did not recognize her; but she did him. It was the rude young man who had without a by-your-leave commandeered the hackney coach that she believed to have been hers, and then had not even offered to help her on her way!

CHAPTER SIX

The very next day they paid a call on Mrs., now Lady, Valerie Forbes at her home on Prospect Lane overlooking St. James Park. It was only a few roads away from Curzon Street and Mayfair where Aunt Judith lived and so, as the rain had ceased and the weather was balmy and beautiful, they decided to walk part of the way with the carriage following behind them. If the roads proved unassailable, they would get into it and be driven the balance of the distance; if not, if the way was clear, they would continue to walk and the carriage could wait to take them home. In that way, Aunt Judith had said, Charlotte would get to see some of the finer homes and have a little fresh air as well. "I'm sure only two days away from Suffolk and you are already longing for a tramp through the greenery."

"Yes, I do like to walk. But as the Forbes house is close to St. James Park, I shall undertake to lead the children there as often as possible." She added, "Providing I am suitable for the position."

"You will be, my dear, I assure you. This call is a mere formality. Lady Forbes, I believe, is aware of her good fortune and will make the most of it."

They had only gone a few yards from Curzon Street when it became clear that they would need the carriage and so they waited until it caught up with them and then climbed aboard. Aunt Judith smiled at Charlotte, "Well it was a good idea, but one has to get used to the fact that after it rains for any appreciable time in London one simply cannot walk anywhere. I hope your boots are not too muddy."

Charlotte laughed. "Not by Suffolk standards."

"Suffolk standards will do, my dear. Just remain your

Suffolk self and nothing in London can harm you. The worst mistakes are made by country folk who try to ape the airs of the city. It never works. Be yourself, Charlotte, and everyone will respect and love you."

"I could never be anything but myself, Aunt. You know that."

"That's true. By the way, you didn't mention anything about home. How is everybody?"

"Dunreath did not look well again, I thought, but she swears she will be up and in London in a few weeks, when Uncle George comes."

"I worry about her so, but there is really nothing we can do. We have had her to the best physicians in London. And Jack and Alfie?"

"I only saw Alfie briefly. He was disappointed that G.H. hadn't come to visit with Anne and me. He seemed in good spirits. Jack was very pleasant and quiet. He, too, longs to come to London. No doubt when Uncle George and Dunreath . . ."

"I don't like it when he comes, Charlotte, I confess, he worries me in a different way. London is too . . . he is too free here. He mixes with all the wrong people. Oh, I don't mean the *demi-monde*, but the worst rakes and dandies, even though they are *of* society. I wish he would stay in Suffolk and settle down." Noticing that Charlotte was reddening, Aunt Judith tactfully changed the subject. Charlotte would be the perfect wife for her son, she thought. But would he be the perfect husband for her?

"And your uncle? He was feeling well?"

"Oh, yes, in very good spirits. He seems the most relaxed person I know. Even more so than my own father."

"Yes, George is a calm man—except when aroused. I'm grateful you've never been around to see him angry. When his wrath is raised . . . I do believe we are here. Yes, this is Prospect Lane. Are the homes not beautiful?"

Indeed they were, all relatively new or newly renovated, built on slight rises so that they looked out to St. James Park. As was the fashion of the city, there was not much space between them, but each had a lawn in front where beautiful flowers had been planted and were even now being tended by gardeners, and of course there was land behind where flowers and trees flourished and where the owners could, if they chose, stroll through arbors without being seen by anyone passing in front. Not that Prospect Lane was a crowded or busy street. But just below it, where it angled into the carriage path around the Park, one could see coaches and hackneys and individuals astride horses. A few strollers, careful to stay away from the muddy portions of the path sauntered along, stopping to talk, to bow and curtsy, to pass the time of day, exchange gossip, and then move on. Prospect Lane overlooked it all, and yet was apart from it, as though it was too perfect, too sedate, to need the rest of London.

"The house across there belongs to Lady Dorothea Chamberley; I believe it was her daughter that Miss Forbes was speaking of yesterday. Lucy. But if you are wise, my dear, although you will be unable not to hear the gossip of the town, you will put as much of it out of your head as possible. For one thing, a great deal of it is not true—or only partially true. And what is true, is rather sordid, I should say and not worthy of you. But it is the habit of London society, its one great pleasure and you must learn to live with it. . . ."

"Taking care," Charlotte interrupted, "to be sure not to be the one being gossipped about."

"By all means. But I think you will find, if Miss Forbes is anywhere near in the right, that you are going to have your hands full with the two children. By the way, how did you like her brother, Rawley?"

"He seemed pleasant enough. I hardly spoke with him." Charlotte had resolved that she would never mention to anyone her unfortunate encounter with Mr. Forbes at the hostelry, especially as it was quite apparent that he did not recognize her. It was best to forget such things, to show a little Christian charity. He had been in a hurry, late for an engagement with his sister, frustrated. It was probably that he just wasn't thinking; had he been, he would surely have offered her transportation. Of course, what he said about the rain and farmers, that had been annoying, too, but she had not taken it in bad part for he had been merely complaining as people often do when caught in a rainstorm without adequate protection.

"Yes, well I doubt that you'll see much of him at home; they say he spends a great deal of time in gaming houses. He has made a few notorious friends, I gather, but his father's money counts for quite a lot. Now, I shall indulge in that very gossip I abhor. Sir James Forbes, it is rumored, got the garter because he had loaned Prinny a considerable sum at an unusually low interest rate."

"Prinny?"

"Oh, the London way. The Prince. Our Regent. Always in debt, worried about Parliament, not really in charge, yet responsible for everything that goes wrong. Well, if it is true, young Rawley Forbes is in an advantageous position, but he is someone I should think you would be better off having as little contact with as possible. No doubt he's a good boy, at heart, and no doubt he'll ignore you almost completely. But just be advised. Perhaps the gossip is wrong. I would not have told you except that I do believe, Charlotte, that forewarned is forearmed."

"I assure you, Aunt Judith, I will have no difficulty at all in heeding your advice. I shall not gossip, nor listen to any more than I absolutely must—and I will stay well clear of Mr. Rawley Forbes, who did not impress me that much anyway."

This was not quite the truth. Despite her annoyance with him, she could not help but notice that he was extremely good-looking; that he carried himself in an easy, indolent way; that he spoke well; and, aside from his failure over the hackney, seemed to possess good manners. There was a supercilious air about him, it was true, but Charlotte put that down to London, supposing (not incorrectly) that most young men of fashion behaved as he did.

Nevertheless, she resolved to put him from her mind.

Lady Forbes was most gracious. She greeted Charlotte and Aunt Judith warmly, especially Charlotte. She was a bit younger than Charlotte had expected, hardly more than thirty, and she explained that her husband was considerably older than she, that they had two children, a boy aged eleven, named after his father, James, and a girl nine, Lisette. Lady Forbes was rather thin and she had dark circles under her eyes as though she did not sleep well. Her hair was a brownish hue, rather colorless and pushed high on her head. Her skin was sallow and her features sharp. She smiled a lot and was not in the least bit unpleasant, but she seemed tense and whenever she spoke of the children it was as if she was speaking of two creatures from across the sea. Her hands shook as she served tea, it was almost as if she were worried that she would not make a good impression on Charlotte rather than the other way round. For some reason, despite her husband's great wealth and her newly found social position, she looked and acted harried and ill-at-ease.

Aunt Judith, sensing that their hostess was uncomfortable, suggested that perhaps the children would like to meet Charlotte and that she, in turn, would certainly like to meet them. This seemed to disconcert Lady Forbes even more, and she asked that they first finish their tea and conversation for, as she put it, the children were apt to be a bit rowdy at tea time, especially with strangers about.

Charlotte, to be polite, asked about their schooling, and who had been caring for them and about their upbringing until now.

"There have been a succession of governesses. Frankly, Miss Linton, we have not made happy choices. James just doesn't want to be bothered—he is such a busy man—and it has all been left in my hands. I believe that the women I chose were all good women, they had good references, but perhaps they were not strong enough of personality, no, perhaps they were a bit too old to cope with two such— how shall I put it?—exuberant children. I am not always able to help. I suffer from the megrim often and have to take to my bed. Then, too, having Rawley and Angelique about has not been ideal for discipline. Angelique is very distant and Rawley is either rude to them or else he spoils them terribly. They have grown up rather wild, I fear. I hope, er, that it will not be too great an undertaking. I mean, if you are willing to undertake the task . . . I contemplated telling you that they were absolutely perfect until you had agreed to take the position, but it would have been of no use, for within minutes you would have seen . . ."

It almost seemed as if Lady Forbes were going to cry. But she didn't. Instead she asked, "More tea?"

As Charlotte passed her cup, she said, "Perhaps it is merely that there is no set schedule, no organization. Children often want to be told what to do. I know with my sisters at home, and G.H., too, he's my brother, when I was left to care for them it was necessary that they understood exactly how much I would tolerate. And what I expected of them."

"Yes, well, I suppose if one is used to doing that sort of thing . . . I am afraid I just can't exercise any sort of discipline. I will leave that up to you. And I promise not to interfere." Her face became stern. "Nor will my husband. In the past, although he would have nothing to do with their rearing, he would suddenly interfere, countermand the poor soul who was trying her best to care for them. We lost one woman that way. The others . . ." her voice trailed off, "just left."

"Well, I promise you that I won't 'just leave,' that is, if you will have me?"

"Oh, my dear, have you? I have been dying for you to come. If you could start this instant, I would be forever grateful. I know you can't. Your Aunt has indicated that you will want a few days to acclimate yourself and to shop, but the sooner the better. Oh, the position is yours, my dear Miss Linton, if you will only take it. I promise you my husband will provide more than adequate compensation, too. I hope I did not give the impression that there was any doubt. . . ."

Charlotte, seeing Lady Forbes's confusion and embarrassment, said quickly, "I will be delighted to take the position. And, if it is absolutely necessary, I could start the day after tomorrow."

"Oh, could you? How wonderful! James will be pleased, too. He has been complaining, nagging me to hire someone, anyone. He is very tense these days. Being knighted was such an honor, but such responsibility goes with it, and he is busy all the time. . . ."

"I'm sure," Charlotte murmured.

"Perhaps Charlotte and I should be leaving now, Lady Forbes."

"Oh, do call me Valerie. I feel so foolish. . . . James revels in it, but I really don't want anyone to think . . . after all . . . well, I would rather . . . you understand. But before you go—the children. You must meet the children. Miss Linton must. I'll get . . . send for them."

She raised the little bell on the tea table and shook it several times. Almost at once a maid appeared. "No, don't take the tea things, Beth. Would you ask the children to come in. There is someone I should like them to meet. I believe they are in the garden. Oh, Beth, this is Miss Linton who will be in charge of them beginning . . . when she comes, the day after tomorrow."

"Pleased, Miss, I'm sure. I hope you'll . . . I wish you well." Her face suggested that Charlotte had a difficult task before her.

"How do you do, Beth. I have a sister at home named Beth. Elizabeth. She's a twin. She's nine."

"I'm an Elizabeth, but not a twin. And I'm sixteen."

"I have a sister who is sixteen, too. Anne. I hope we shall be friends, Beth."

"Anything, I can do to help, Miss."

"My name is Charlotte. You can call me that. I really prefer it. Perhaps not in front of the children, not at first, anyway." Charlotte was beginning to have an idea. Small rewards for good behavior. They could start off calling her Miss Linton and could perhaps graduate to Charlotte.

"I'll get them," Beth said, rather grimly.

Lady Forbes sat apprehensively, attempting a little smile, several times acting as though she were either going to start a conversation or bolt from the room, it was hard to tell which, for she would suddenly sit upright and then relax again into her chair.

"Your home is quite lovely," Charlotte said.

"Yes, thank you. We . . . we like it very much. We only purchased it last year. Lady Chamberley lives across the way. The same man designed this one as hers. I can't think of his name."

"John Nash," Aunt Judith said. "He visits us often. If you should like to meet him, Lady Forbes . . ."

"Valerie. Yes, I suppose that would be nice. It is a very comfortable house. It requires a large staff, though. James is always complaining that . . . here they come." She sounded almost frightened when she made the announcement of the impending arrival of her offspring.

They seemed to pour into the room. Indeed they *had* been playing out-of-doors, for their clothing was mud-spattered and their shoes even worse. The little girl, thin and pale with wispy blonde hair and rather prominent front teeth, smiled alertly and made an attempt at a curtsy. The boy, larger, dark, and rather sullen-looking, just stood and stared at Charlotte and Aunt Judith for a moment. Then he came into the room and said, "Good. Tea. I'm hungry as a dog. Aren't you, Zette?"

49

"Don't call me that. You know I hate it. In front of strangers."

"Zette! Zette!" he said.

"Juny! Juny!" she replied until he glared at her.

"Children!" Lady Forbes stood up and did her best to take a strong and commanding attitude. "Please mind your manners. This is Mrs. Ellicott. And Miss Linton, who will be coming to stay with us in a day or two. She will be your governess."

"Which one?" the boy asked as he reached for a scone.

With that Charlotte stood up and answered him. "I shall be coming to stay with you starting immediately. I am Miss Linton. I shall be in charge of your education and your manners. We will begin with the manners. Before there will be any tea, we will have clean hands, faces, and boots. Please show me where you can wash."

She took each of them by the arm and before they could answer led them from the room. Had she looked back (fortunately she didn't) she would have seen Lady Forbes collapse back into her chair while Aunt Judith, holding herself in check until the door was closed behind Charlotte and the children, began to laugh.

CHAPTER SEVEN

And so Miss Charlotte Linton came to stay with the family of Sir James and Lady Forbes to attempt to instruct their two children in sums and spelling and reading, but in manners as well. It might be thought by some that country manners are different than city manners, but that is not so. Good manners are more or less the same in the country and the city. True, in the city there is more pomp and ceremony, a superficial layer of politeness often masking cruelty, whereas in the country people are far more open and above-board. But in good families, in good society, a certain code of behavior existed, still exists, and will always exist. It was this code, as well as educational matters, that Charlotte was determined to teach. For, although it came naturally to her, she could see that was as much because of her parents, her relatives and her friends as any special ability on her part. Raised the right way, she decided, you will do the right thing. This, of course, is an oversimplification, but it does generally hold to be true.

Progress was, as she knew it would be, slow, but within a week they were, to her mind, at least physically presentable. That is, they washed themselves each morning and evening, bathed on Saturday, and remembered to wash their hands before each meal. Also, they took to keeping their clothes (their wardrobes were unbelievably extensive) in a somewhat neater fashion. Indeed, they looked a lot better, but sadly, they did not behave that much better, at least by her standards. But always the optimist, she told herself, one thing at a time. We have made a beginning.

And, she found, despite it all, she was enjoying her position and growing to like the children, no mean task, for both were either recalcitrant and surly or highly emotional and volatile.

What she discovered almost at once was that it was important to keep them active. They had been too long around the house with no real interests, no attention, no opportunity to meet and play with children their own age. She resolved that in a month or two she would, after they were in her opinion more responsive to her, request permission to take them for a visit to Linton Park. But for now, it was necessary to intersperse the lessons with games or activities which used up some of their excess energy so that they could more easily concentrate in the classroom.

She quickly adjusted to the household routine, which she discovered was rather peculiar. Sir James was seldom at home (she had met him only three times). Lady Forbes was often abroad visiting, although she did not have that many visitors herself. And Miss and Mr. Forbes seemed to come and go as they pleased. One day she suggested to Lady Forbes that she would like to take the children to St. James Park for the day, that is, the latter part of the morning, a picnic lunch, and the afternoon. This was most agreeable to the children's mother for she was "at home" that day and hoping to have some visitors, people returning her calls, and the children, even kept far from the drawing room, made her nervous.

Beth was summoned and told to ask the kitchen help to prepare a luncheon basket for three. Then Charlotte suggested that perhaps Beth would like to accompany them. As there were a number of servants, it turned out to be no inconvenience at all, and Beth, in turn, seemed to look forward to an escape from the dull routine of the house. And so, shortly after eleven they set out for the Park, only a few hundred yards away.

Beth was in a holiday mood, which was natural enough and her good nature was infectious so that Lisette who had been rather negative about a picnic on the grass ("Won't there be bugs?") and James, who saw that he was going to spend the day with thre women—something of an affront to his eleven-year-old manhood—soon began to enjoy the stroll down Prospect Lane to St. James Park. It was especially pleasurable when they got to the crossing where so many carriages were driving by at an inordinately slow pace and so many men were riding up and down the path

52

on horseback, peering into the carriages. Even a few strollers, wisely staying far from the carriages and horses, stopped to greet one another. It was said, Beth whispered to Charlotte, that this stretch on the north side of the Park was where lovers made their assignations. She blushed beet-red as she spoke the words, but her eyes were darting everywhere, trying to recognize people or carriages.

Charlotte was more amused than shocked. London society was presumed to be licentious, but she suspected that that was less fact than fancy. Still, she admired the beautifully groomed and trained horses, the gorgeous carriages, with gilt trimmings, coats of arms, and the fine clothing of both the men and women. Now that the men of fashion were wearing trousers rather than breeches, aping their Regent who in turn aped the notorious Mr. Brummell, they looked strange compared to country folk, but rather dashing all the same. And the women all seemed to be beautiful. Certainly they wore the most ornate and lavish hats Charlotte had ever seen.

None of this particularly impressed the children, although James admired the horses and Lisette the hats on the ladies. They waited until the traffic left an opening and then quickly crossed into St. James Park.

There were a number of small paths, shooting off from the main one, and they took one that seemed particularly shady (for it had grown quite warm) and not too busy. They would find a cool glade somewhere, and sit down, spread out their feast and eat; perhaps, if they found high ground, they would even be able to look across the city, see as far as the Thames. Certainly the bridges would be visible as well as the palace and one or two stately monuments.

The Park had a large lake running through its center and they soon found themselves beside it, in a cool, shaded, untrafficked area. They were on low ground and could see little because of the trees, but there was one thing they could see: the spires of Westminster Abbey. It made their little glade almost cathedral-like, Charlotte thought, for she had always been devout and went to services every Sunday in Suffolk. She had been chagrinned that the Forbeses, although professing to be C. of E., did not attend regular services, so her first week with them she went alone to St. Luke's nearby. The children did not accompany her, but she was resolved that the next week they would and all subsequent weeks, for religion, too, should be part of their upbringing.

They found a flat dry section of land a few yards from the lake and Beth spread out the table covering she had brought and then opened the hamper. The children were eager to eat but Charlotte suggested they wait a few minutes. As they sat there, a punt came by with a young man and young lady, she demurely shading herself from the sun and anyone on land who might recognize her with a parasol, he poling easily in the still waters. James and Lisette waved and he gave them a half-hearted salute in return, not wanting to lose the grip on the pole.

"That looks like ever so much fun," Lisette said.

"Yes," her brother replied, "for the passenger."

"Oh, I shouldn't mind poling it."

"Punting its called. Not poling."

"Whatever it's called, I shouldn't mind."

"But the man is supposed to do it."

"Very well, then," his sister replied logically, "you may do it and I shall ride in the front and dangle my hand in the water and watch you sweat."

"Perspire," Charlotte said. "People perspire. Animals sweat."

"Well, he's an . . ."

"Never mind," Charlotte interrupted. "Perhaps later we can find a place where they rent punts and we'll all go. In two punts, of course."

That seemed to mollify them for the moment and both children moved down to the bank to see if any more punts were in sight.

"It was kind of you, Miss, to invite me," Beth said.

"Now you must call me Charlotte—when they're not about. It wasn't kind. I wanted the company. I miss my own sister and my cousin. My closest sister is your age and my cousin, Dunreath is mine. I'm used to having someone to talk to my own age as well as having younger ones about. Then, too, I could always talk to my mother and Aunt Judith. In this household . . ." She stopped, not wanting to be guilty of gossiping.

"I know what you mean. They are very strange. It is my first position so I don't have anything to compare them with, but some of the others say . . . well, they say strange things about them."

Charlotte was curious, but she forbore asking the question she knew Beth wanted her to ask.

Beth began to set out some food and as she did she talked. "What they say below stairs is that they had very little until just a few years ago. Mr. Forbes—excuse me, Sir James—speculated, whatever that is, invested wildly I think someone called it and it paid off handsomely. Until then, no one even recognized them." She looked up to see if Charlotte was listening.

Charlotte was watching the children, torn between suggesting that it might be better if Beth were not to tell her these things and wanting to know, not just out of idle curiosity, but because she too could not fathom the behavior of the family and that, of course, affected her responsibilities, the caring for the children. Besides, she told herself, there was nothing wrong with earning money and getting a better house, making new friends. Everyone couldn't remain the same forever. Things shifted in nature, why not in society? Still, she said nothing, deciding that if Beth stopped she would not press her, but if she continued she would not stop her either.

"I don't understand much about it, but they were sort of trying to get into society, that's what Kelsey, the butler says, and not doing too well, not being invited to any of the posh places and then, so he says, one night something happened and Sir James got to meet the Prince and they were drinking and he pledged a loan to the Prince. Evidently he didn't have it and Mrs. Forbes had a fit and they were very upset and that day he went out, plunged all that he had on the bourse, and somehow or other he made a big profit. Now that's what I hear, Miss and I don't know that it is true, but ever since then their fortunes have just gone up and up. People talk about them behind their backs, but because the Prince invites them everywhere, they can't quite be ignored. So Kelsey says."

"I think I should call the children to eat."

"Yes, it's all ready. There is just one other thing. None of them is happy, have you noticed?"

With that thought buzzing in her head, Charlotte called out, "Lisette! James! Come and eat. Then we shall walk along the lake and look for the place where they hire the punts."

The children came at once, not so much because they

55

had learned to obey as because they were hungry and what had been prepared for the outing promised to be a feast indeed.

They wanted to eat right away but Charlotte first checked their hands, mercifully clean for a change, and then made them sit properly and be served. When they had their plates in front of them, Charlotte bowed her head and asked a brief blessing followed by an "Amen." The children looked at her as if she had two heads but said nothing. Beth added an "Amen" herself in a ghostly quiet voice.

Cheerfully Charlotte said, "It can't hurt to ask the Lord's blessing, can it, nor thank Him for His bounty? We do it at home all the time."

"Tis Popish," James said.

"Nonsense. Romans are not the only ones to ask Grace. You don't have to do it and I know your parents don't at their table, but while we are on this outing we are at my table and we follow my customs. It is a good rule. When in Rome do as the Romans do."

"You see. Popish."

"Rome was also a country—that is a city-state, and the expression only means to follow the custom of the place where you are. Often you will be invited out and the custom in a particular home may be different than your own, so you follow the custom of the host. That is good manners."

"Can we eat now?" he asked.

"You *can* always eat. Now you *may* eat. And pass me a napkin, please. Beth has set us a glorious table, but the cloths are still by the hamper."

Beth started to get up but Charlotte quickly told her to sit, that Lisette was closer and she, Beth, was one of them for the afternoon and had already done enough, preparing the places, and arranging the viands on the plates.

Lisette passed the napkins and resumed her seat. They all fell to with hearty appetites and there was very little conversation for the first few minutes of the meal. It was only after James, having emptied his plate and asked for more, that Charlotte suggested that in polite society conversation took place during the eating of the meal and that he could have more, provided he led them in any topic of his choice.

He was nonplussed for a moment and then he assented, filling his plate and sitting down cross-legged on the grass. "The topic for discussion is my cousin, Rawley Forbes."

"Well, I don't know that we should discuss personalities."

"You said any topic of my choice. I like Rawley—most of the time. I shall not say anything too bad about him. But don't you think he is interesting? Besides, there are all women here, it makes me feel better to talk about a man."

He's rather precocious, Charlotte thought. More so than I imagined. Well, I'll indulge his whim, then. "Go ahead," she said. "What would you like to say about Mr. Forbes?"

Challenged as it were, James grew silent for a moment. He *had* wanted to talk about Rawley, to dominate the conversation, but just now he felt tongue-tied. The problem was he had picked a subject about which he really didn't have much to say. Rawley, whom he admired so much at times and then, when Rawley was being particularly beastly, loathed with equal fervor, was an enigma to him.

They were all looking at him, so he felt he had to say something, especially as Lisette was smirking in that way of hers that always made him feel the fool.

"I know something about him that no one else knows," he said.

"Well, if it is private, something that shouldn't be known by others, then it would be best if you didn't repeat it. One must never, never tell tales on others, James."

"I want to know what it is," Lisette said.

"It isn't really a secret, I don't think. It's not exactly bad, I mean he didn't do something dishonorable exactly."

"Even so, it might be better . . ." Charlotte was saying.

"But it did make Father very angry."

"Well, then, you definitely . . ."

"Oh, what was it?" Lisette wailed. "You always tease, James." When she wanted something from him she called him by his right name. It was only when she was hurt or angry or trying to get even that she called him "Juny."

"It isn't as serious as all that. He told me. Well he didn't exactly tell me in so many words, but I heard him talking to Father and then he said that it was all right if I knew."

"Didn't he also tell you not to repeat it?" Charlotte asked.

"No. He just laughed and said that everything would be all right and that Father just didn't understand. Not to worry."

There was a long silence. Lisette looked at her brother imploringly. Beth busied herself with the food and Charlotte waited to see what he would do. She wasn't sure what he was going to say, certainly wasn't sure that she wanted to hear it, yet on the other hand, it was probably something innocuous and it was one of the few times that James had spoken in her presence in anything more than monosyllables and grunts.

Finally he spoke. "Rawley challenged someone to a duel and they were going to fight at dawn or something with pistols only the other fellow's seconds came round and it all got straightened out. I guess they apologized or something. Anyway, Rawley thinks it is a great lark and Father is angry and they say that Prinny even has heard about it, but no one knows if *he* is angry or thinks it's a lark. Rawley only hopes . . . well, he would like to be invited . . . Prinny is going hunting next month somewhere up north."

CHAPTER EIGHT

The subject of their discussion was at that point not far away, although they were not aware of his presence, nor he of theirs. As they were eating and chatting, he was engaged in a conversation of his own with a lady a few years older than himself, and one that was married to boot. To her it was an innocent flirtation, for she enjoyed having beaux about, young men who inevitably, because of her rather remarkable beauty, fell in love with her. To him, it was serious. It was, in fact, because of her that he had issued the challenge to a duel, a challenge that was foolish, quickly hushed up and hopefully soon forgotten. There would be no duel at any rate, and although Rawley Forbes was rather full of himself, he supposed he was just as happy that he had not had to go through with it. If, even by accident, he were to die . . . ! Well, the thought was unthinkable.

Fortunately the lady in question, the one in whose coach he was now sitting while one of her footmen held his horse, did not know of the near-escapade. Or if she did, she chose not to let him know that she knew. He rather amused her. He had more money than sense, she supposed, and that was what she liked. Her husband, who was considerably older than she, had a great deal of sense and a great deal of money, but his great deal of sense kept him from parting with more than a slight bit of his money, and she rather liked pretty things.

As a matter of fact, Rawley Forbes was a pretty thing and she enjoyed his attentions. She also was aware of his intentions but she was not about to have any real scandal come to her name. Flirtation did not cause scandal. She would know exactly the right time to send him packing. In the meantime, Sophia Kent-Chillingham would enjoy his company, allow him to squire her about, and accept such tokens of his esteem as he chose to give. Her husband understood the rules, and as long as things did not get out of hand, Gerald Kent-Chillingham was content to let Sophia live her own life as he led his. But he had warned her several years ago that there must be no hint of real scandal attached to his old and venerable name. That was why several wise people saw that the challenge was refused and hushed up quickly. No scandal. So far Sophia had played by his rules. Rawley Forbes, somewhat an innocent in the ways of London society, did not understand any of this. He thought he was in love. It mattered not that the lady was married and six years older than himself. He had the confidence of youth.

So he dallied in her carriage, passing effusive compliments, using the affected drawl that was so the rage in London as he leaned back opposite her. She in turn sat out of sight in the far end of the coach and bantered with him, teased him, asking for the latest gossip, of which she no doubt knew much more than he.

He was content to stay this way for the day, but she wished, she said, to go shopping. He offered to accompany her. She demurred. It would look too forward. Besides, gentlemen were uncomfortable in ladies shops. True, he responded, then why not have the coachman drive them a few times about the park, to take the air and see who else was about. She agreed, so long as it did not take too long. He gave the order to her driver and then returned inside to sit beside her. Aware of his ruse, she didn't shrink away but rather moved a little closer so that he could take her hand in his.

He would want to kiss her, she was sure. So far she had kept him at bay. Today she would allow him that liberty. Then she would change her mind and allow him to shop with her. There was a new dress that she coveted. She did not have her purse. He would be most gallant. After all, he was rich, they said. Or his older cousin was. It would be from her point of view a perfect day. A harmless stolen kiss, a soulful look into his eyes, and a new dress.

The coach began the rounds. Passers-by peered inside but they could see only dark shadows. A few recognized the carriage as belonging to the Marquis of Kent-

Chillingham, but who was inside was another matter. No doubt the Marchioness, but who was she with? Or was she alone? It didn't cause undue attention, though, for there were many such carriages circling St. James Park and often as not nothing of great import could be inferred from what was seen.

"Would you like to punt?" he asked.

"What?"

"There is a place nearby where one can rent a punt. It is such a lovely day, I thought we might take to the lake, drift along among the lilies, under the trees, for an hour or so."

The idea intrigued her. "Perhaps for a short time. Do you think I'll be recognized?"

"There is no one about. You have your parasol." He moved closer. "Do say 'yes.' I should like it so."

"Yes to what? Punting or something else?"

"Would it be too forward if I were to kiss you?"

"Yes. But you may if you like."

For Sophia it was not an unpleasant experience but it meant nothing. For Rawley Forbes, it was almost as though he had died and gone to heaven. And he had the punting to look forward to as well. There would be a place, somewhere in the overhanging of the willows where they could moor, step out onto the fresh grass . . . His quest was almost over.

He had the carriage stop and he got out, walked down the path, and made arrangements for a punt. There was, as he had said, no one about. He came back for her, took her by the hand, led her down the same path, and helped her into the squat, flat-bottomed boat. Then he grasped the pole, stepped aboard, and shoved off. He anticipated no trouble for he was quite athletic and he had done the same thing before, always with a female passenger.

It was indeed peaceful on the lake and there were hardly any other punters to be seen and they at great distance; nor were the banks lined with people and by keeping to the center (it made punting a bit harder) they were practically assured of not being recognized if that was her worry. He didn't care so much, in fact it would be a feather in his cap, he supposed, if he *were* recognized—that is, recognized with this particular lady. Still, he didn't want to do anything to disturb her calm. She sat in the front, shading her head from the glare of the sun and watching his wrists and arms bulge as he pushed the heavy pole into the sludgy bottom of the lake.

He was certainly a handsome lad, far more athletic than her husband. But she was not going to entertain such thoughts; her life was far too perfect to let it get out of hand by allowing too many liberties to a young man of questionable birth who simply happened to be related to a man who had made money and to whom Prinny was beholden. Such men as Mr. Rawley Forbes were excellent as lap dogs, to be petted and pampered a little, but good for nothing more. No, if she were going to fall (and she wasn't, she saw no need to) it would be for someone far more debonair, even richer, and with more—not less—power than her husband. In the meantime, Mr. Forbes provided an interesting *divertissement*.

He punted for a while, whistling softly. He could feel the perspiration on his back and forehead, and so, once they were midstream, he relaxed and let the punt drift. It was heading in the general direction he had in mind, a place where the man-made lake narrowed and where there was plenty of seclusion.

Slowly the current took them to a narrower part of the lake and ultimately close to the shore line where the sun was not so visible and the leaves from the trees made dappled shadows on her dress and the punt.

"We seem to have come to the end of the lake," she said.

"Oh, no. The stream narrows here, but you can get through. There is a wider section just beyond. Unless you'd like to land here for a few minutes."

"Tired?"

"Well, the old arms aren't quite used to this sort of thing."

"You seem to know your way through the maze, though."

"Well, we live close by. I have been here before, I confess."

"Alone?"

"Uh, not always."

"I see. No, I think perhaps we should go back. I don't want to be gone too long. You know how the servants gossip."

"Oh, very well. If I can get us turned around."

"That shouldn't be too hard, if you're really experienced."

"Look, Sophia, wouldn't you like to step out onto land for just a few minutes. It is quite beautiful. Also it would be easier to get about. I'm rather stuck here."

"Oh, very well, you naughty boy. But only for a minute, mind you."

While they were climbing carefully from the punt onto dry land, only a short distance away the party of four was finishing its picnic luncheon.

"Shall we play a game?" Charlotte suggested.

"I'd rather sleep," James said.

"No. I want to play," Lisette countered. "Let's play hide-and-seek. We'll all hide and Charlotte can be 'it'."

"Fine. We play that at home all the time. I'm good at it. But we must have some rules. You can't just hide anywhere. The Park is too big."

"Fine," James said. "I'll go hide behind this tree and sleep."

"No, we have to be serious. Anywhere from here to the lake but not beyond that stand of trees over there and not beyond the curve of the bank in the other direction. That leaves us plenty of room. Go ahead, the three of you, hide. I'll count to a hundred."

Charlotte put her head down and started to count slowly. Beth and Lisette hurried off while James, with a simulated groan, stood up, yawned, and walked away whistling. He didn't want to play, she understood that, but at the same time he didn't want to be the first one caught and have to be 'it', so she imagined he would find a pretty good place, probably up in a tree.

When she finished counting she opened her eyes and looked warily around. Of course none of them was in sight. She rather guessed that they had split up, although Lisette may have tried to stay fairly close to Beth. Charlotte walked a little ways in one direction, staring carefully at the trees, and then came back and went the other way. Nothing seemed to be stirring. She decided that the most likely place was the stand of trees down by the lake where it narrowed to a few feet in breadth and then widened again on the other side of the passage way. Those trees would provide the best cover for anyone wishing to remain unseen from the hillock or even from the lake itself. Yes, the children and Beth were sure to be there.

Gingerly she moved forward. Although she could not see them, if they were watching closely they could see her, and perhaps change their positions before she reached their original hiding place.

She decided not to make a frontal attack but rather to skirt the trees as though she were going to the far side of them, edging closer all the time and then, just as they had done so often at Linton Park, with a burst of speed, run right into the center of the grove where she was sure she would find at least one of them. It was a strategy she was familiar with, for it was a game they played seemingly for hours on end at home, a game for children of all ages from her twin sisters, who were Lisette's age, through G.H., just a little older than James, up to Anne, comparable to Beth in years, and finally herself.

Out of the corner of her eye she saw something move back in the other direction. Quickly she changed her plans and went back toward the blanket, the starting place. Down near the curve in the bank were a few rocks and some scrub bushes. She had seen someone there. Whoever it was, that person was trapped. Then there was movement again and she recognized the pale yellow of Lisette's dress. No, she didn't want to catch Lisette first. She was the youngest and the easiest. And Charlotte remembered how at home their Beth was always upset when she was made 'it', and she and Lisette were the same age.

She watched for a moment and then turned away and started back toward the stand of trees. There was definitely movement down there; she could see some flashes of color but she could not tell whether it was James or Beth or both of them. Again she took the indirect route, deliberately moving above and slightly beyond the trees, in order to outflank whoever it might be. If she caught them both at once, that would make Lisette doubly happy.

Beth wouldn't care and neither would James, really, except that he would lose face in front of his little sister. Well, that would be good for him. Casually she looked around as though she could not imagine where anyone might be hiding.

Yes, there was definitely someone there, two people most likely. Slowly she began to creep up on them.

There were actually three people. James was, as Charlotte had first guessed, up in a tree. And perched in that tree he was looking down on his cousin, Rawley, and a woman he had never seen before. Rawley was embracing the woman and she was struggling slightly, not exactly resisting but not allowing herself to be lowered to the ground. James didn't know precisely what it all meant, but he knew that if Rawley should see him there he would be in for it. So he kept very quiet. By now he had forgotton completely about the game of hide-and-seek, so interesting was the scene before him.

The lady was laughing, but his cousin, he could see, was red-faced and rather annoyed. She had slipped away from him and she stood a little distance with her hands held out before her. "Now, Mr. Forbes," she was saying, "I must ask you to behave like a gentleman. Really, what would people say! I am, after all, a respectable married woman. I don't mind an embrace now and then to show affection, but as for the other little familiarities, I think it would be better if you remember that ladies of quality are not so easily won over as the little shop girls you have no doubt taken punting in the past." In this remark she hit home and Rawley's face reddened even more. "A harmless flirtation, sir, is all I expected. Now, I think we should return to the punt and then to my carriage. We have been gone quite long enough."

"I apologize, but I was sure . . . damn, if I understand, Sophia. You have been most obliging and I thought we were getting to know one another and . . ."

"Yes, well, perhaps, dear boy, some day we shall, but I hardly think that you should expect to take liberties until I have quite made it clear that I feel we have been friends long enough. You are young, dear boy, and I do forgive you. You must not look so hang-dog. It is all right. But you must not presume . . ." Sophia Kent-Chillingham was certain the new dress was as good as hers. It hadn't really been a close call, she had been in control of the situation all the way, but he was rather impetuous and had she let him he would have thrown her to the turf. Outrageous. No breeding. Still, he was rather charming, standing there embarrassed. And he was strong and manly. It had not been totally unpleasant at all. But hardly the time or the place.

Again he apologized. "I am most dreadfully sorry. I took

it for granted . . . I promise never to make the same mistake again. I will wait patiently."

"Of course. I understand. You must learn patience. Some day, perhaps, but at the moment my life is so confused. I know I should be quite angry with you, darling boy, but I can't, somehow. Now don't look like a dog whose master has just beaten him. It will be all right. Straighten your coat. There, do I look all right? Good. Now, we should return. Come here, I'll straighten your cravat for you. There's my good boy."

Shyly he came to her and James leaned far out on the branch, for now they were just below him.

The young lady brushed off his coat, gave it a couple of tugs, and then turned Rawley Forbes around so that he was facing her.

"Just to show that there are no ill feelings, you may kiss me once more. A trifle less enthusiastically this time, if you please. And then we must hurry for I have shopping to do. You may accompany me if you like."

She tilted her head upward toward his face and Rawley Forbes, thoroughly chastened, bent over her and pressed his lips lightly against hers just as Charlotte Linton came through the trees calling out, "Caught you! You're it!"

James, unable to believe his ears, or see what was happening, leaned too far forward and fell out of the tree at the feet of his cousin and the attractive lady.

CHAPTER NINE

It was a most impossible situation and easily the most embarrassing one of her life. Now that it was over, she realized that she had been shaking during the whole confrontation, short as it was. Fortunately James was unhurt, although he did limp around the house for days and he had a badly skinned and bruised elbow. The pain, the real pain, was felt by the other three, especially herself.

She could not, would not, recall his words to her. To say that he was angry was an understatement. He accused her of spying on him. When she tried to explain he simply took the lady and tramped away without introducing her. He ignored completely James, writhing on the ground, crying more from fear of his cousin than from actual physical pain. The lady was red-faced, then she grew very white, her eyes narrowed, and she looked at Charlotte as though she might want her dead, which probably at that moment she did.

She said something about the arrogance of servants, then turned away, walked to the edge of the water, her back to Charlotte. Rawley came back and spitefully demanded that Charlotte leave the Forbes home at once, that if she did not resign, he would see to it that she was sent away at once. He called her a "country snoop," a spy sent by his cousin, a dozen other things. When James tried to explain that they had been playing hide-and-seek, that they had come to St. James Park on a picnic, and that they had no idea . . . Rawley merely walked away from him, threatening to thrash him if he ever breathed a word.

Rawley returned to the lady and helped her into the punt. As he pushed off, he slipped and fell into the water. Both James and Charlotte, although it was unpardonable, laughed. That was the biggest mistake of all. Finally Rawley and the lady were gone. The game of hide-and-seek was definitely over.

Lisette was very curious when she and Beth came in from where they had been hiding, where Lisette had first been seen by Charlotte, but neither James nor Charlotte would say anything. Charlotte simply told them that James had fallen from a tree and hurt himself slightly and it would be best if they were to pack the things up and go home. He would be all right, she was sure, but he should get off of his foot as soon as possible and the wound on his arm should be washed and dressed. Beth scurried about gathering up the food, the blanket, and the utensils and put everything into the hamper, then they started back. Lisette, though, was not totally mollified. She said she heard noises from the stand of trees and she was sure something else had happened.

James glared at her and Charlotte, her face white with rage, for she had never been spoken to in that tone, was silent. She was not going to say anything to Lady Forbes, however, nor was she going to resign, much as she wished to do so. If he chose to make an issue of it (she doubted he would for it would require too much of an explanation of his own injudicious behavior), then she would make her explanation and allow her employer to decide. But no matter what happened, she imagined correctly that she was in for an unpleasant time in the Forbes household, at least whenever Rawley Forbes was present.

When they got back to the house, Lady Forbes was entertaining and so was not to be disturbed. Beth retired to the kitchen and Charlotte took the children upstairs, dressed James's wounds while Lisette watched anxiously and then felt his ankle and had him walk about on it. It was quite clearly not broken, nor even sprained. Falling out of trees had been rather common at Linton Park for both sexes. In fact she, herself, had fallen once when seven or eight and she knew just how to deal with the ankle. She had a maid draw a hot bath and then she added salt to the water and had James sit on the edge of the porcelain tub, the latest innovation (they had nothing like it at home) and dangle his foot in the water. Then the hot water was replaced with cold to remove the swelling. After that she dried and bandaged it and told him that he must be very careful about his movements for a day or two, that it would swell and become discolored and that he would be most comfortable off his feet or, if he had to move around, using a staff or cane. He seemed rather to enjoy the attention. Lisette had watched the whole process, hopeful of gleaning some tidbit of information about the interrupted afternoon, but they said nothing until she finally, in despair and disgust, left for her own room.

Now that they were alone, James looked up at her from his perch on the stool and said, "What shall we do? Rawley is really furious. He might do anything."

"Now don't fret, James. My guess is that he will do and say nothing. First of all, we have to remember that despite his charges, we are totally innocent. We were not following him about, nor spying on him. It was merely an accident that he . . . landed, stopped his punt where you were hiding in the tree."

"I suppose so. I could have warned him, though, climbed down, called out, only I was afraid to."

"Precisely. You did what you thought was best, but you were not deliberately spying. Nor was I. I came upon them by accident. I saw flashes of color and I believed it to be you and Beth. Now, surely, when he thinks it over he will see that we are not at fault. I doubt he wants to be reminded of the incident. Not," she hastened to add, "that we should infer that anything wrong was going on. He was merely on an outing with a young lady, which is perfectly acceptable. We would be best to put it from our minds, certainly to say nothing to anyone, not to your sister or your mother or father or any one of the servants."

"But if he does?"

"We shall cross that bridge when we come to it."

"He won't have you discharged will he?"

"I don't think so. He was angry because he was embarrassed and the young lady was there. After all, I don't even know her and I doubt I shall ever see her again. If I should, I shall act as though nothing has happened and so should you. It was one of those unfortunate incidents. The least said is soonest mended."

"What's that?"

"A country saying. The less you say about something the sooner it is forgotten. It would be best for all of us if we forget it as soon as possible."

"It was jolly funny when he fell into the drink. I hated to laugh, but I couldn't help myself."

"No, we should not have laughed, but we did and there is an end to it. We will not discuss it again and we will wait and see. Hopefully your cousin will be equally determined to drop the topic entirely."

That was, and yet was not, quite the case. His rage didn't leave him as Rawley Forbes poled the punt back across the lake. Sophia had her back to him and was, he could tell, most angry. It was one thing to have been discovered (that was bad enough!), but to have been discovered by members of his own household, that was too much. He was quite certain she would never wish to lay eyes on him again. And to have been such a fool as to have fallen into the muddy bottom in front of all of them—in front of her! She had to think him a complete ass. He poled harder. Someone would pay for this ignominy.

When they reached the other side of the lake, Sophia Kent-Chillingham allowed the boat boy to help her out of the punt and without looking behind her, she headed straight up the path for her carriage. Rawley, miserable, but determined to make amends, payed the boy and brushing off the muck as best he could from his trousers, hurried after her. She was already stepping into her carriage when he reached the top of the path.

"Sophia," he called. "Please wait. Let me explain."

"You surely don't think that you *can* explain. What is there to say? I depended on you and you did not know what you were doing. Besides, I hardly want some mud-splattered ruffian seen with me in my carriage."

"Please, Sophia, I am so sorry. Let me come with you and try to explain—to make amends."

"Oh, very well. Climb in. But sit as far away from me as possible. And out of sight. I must stop at several places. I've shopping to do, as I told you. But you will not, I repeat, you will *not* attempt to accompany me inside. I will let you out on some dark byway."

"Oh, thank you Sophia. Can your man take my horse to the stable? That way, no one will know. . . ."

"Excellent idea. But I shan't be able to drive you home. I have much too much to do."

"It doesn't matter. Just to be with you, to know you are not angry with me."

"But I am angry with you. However, I shan't leave you here in that condition. Get in but don't waste time with explanations. Just make sure that I never see that child—or that young woman again. Who is she, anyway? Another relation?"

"No, she is nothing more than a servant. From somewhere up north. I don't know where Valerie found her—wait, yes, I do. She is related to someone, to Lady Fitzhugh, a distant connection, no doubt, and the old lady was doing her a favor. I've hardly seen her. Supposed to be teaching the little monsters good manners. Teaching him to spy from a tree. Well, she'll hear from me, you can be sure, and so shall my cousin."

"I can't say I blame you for being angry, Rawley. That sort of person, no real breeding. Whatever she was doing, she wasn't minding her place. One can't have that. I don't care what you do, but it would be most embarrassing for me if I were to set eyes on her again."

There, she thought, that would take care of the country cousin. Rawley would have her packed off to her north country home in no time. At least he had better. Sophia certainly didn't want word of the incident to get around. Her husband, especially, must not know that she was punting with Rawley Forbes. And of course the stupid girl and the clumsy child saw them embracing. . . . The child may have seen more . . . well, not really more, for nothing had actually happened, but there had been an earlier embrace, less chaste, perhaps, less controlled. Could the girl have been skulking about then? No, she would definitely have to go. The boy would be less of a problem. He was obviously terrified of Rawley.

The carriage had pulled away from the Park and was now making its way slowly through the London afternoon traffic to the center of the city where she would do her shopping. She hoped that the dress she so coveted was finished and she was sure it would be paid for that very day, unless the clod had lost his purse when he fell in the water.

After they had pulled over so that she could step down, he said, "Am I forgiven, Sophia? I really had no idea. . . ."

"We shall see. Now you wait here and stay out of sight. I

71

shall be quite a while so do not get impatient, and for the sake of all I hold dear, do not draw attention to yourself. If you do, then I promise you, I will never, never see you again."

"I promise you. I'll wait and say nothing, do nothing."

"Good." She stepped outside and out of his line of vision. He assumed she had gone into some shop or other, but he dared not look. He felt such a fool but he could not help himself. He supposed he was in love.

Now, while he was alone, waiting for her (and experience had taught him that no matter how much he might wish otherwise, it would not be a short wait), he would try to decide how best to approach the problem of the troublesome Miss Linton. He hardly knew her, but he knew he didn't like her. And that had nothing to do with the incident that afternoon by the lake. There was something about her. The children already liked her, not that he cared that much for them, he supposed, yet he was rather fond of them, most of the time. And they of him. Well, never mind, that wasn't important now. What was important was that Miss Linton would have to go. Sophia had decreed it.

A short while ago it had not seemed to be a problem at all. In fact when he had been first discovered he had threatened to have her dismissed and, of course, then he had intended to make good on his threat. But thinking on it, there were problems. Valerie liked her and the children liked her. And she was related to Lady Fitzhugh, who might be offended. And then there was Angelique—not quite betrothed to the oaf Cedric, but still a match might be in the offing. He would have to proceed a bit more cautiously than he had first thought.

There must be a way, he told himself. Perhaps he could talk to the girl, offer her something, some money, if only she would be gone. Perhaps he could explain to her. No that would never do; he could tell her type. She would judge him a rake, a philanderer. She already thought him a dandy, it was clear from the way she appraised his fashionable dress. At first he had thought she was admiring him, but then it occurred to him that she disapproved. There was something else, too. She kept looking at him as if they had met before. She did look vaguely familiar, but he had never been north and he was sure she had never been to any place of importance in London.

72

Still, she would have to be dealt with. But how?

While he was trying desperately to come up with a solution, Sophia Kent-Chillingham was having the last fitting on the dress she had ordered without her husband's knowledge. A few stitches and it would be ready. She could take it with her. But it would be wise that she pay for it. A bill to her husband at this particular time would not be appreciated. "Wrap it carefully," she said, "I'll be right back."

It was hot on the street. Her carriage horses flicked away flies with their tails. The driver, since the footman had been sent off with Mr. Forbes's horse, sat up above, half-asleep. He didn't notice her return to the carriage, nor her light tapping on the door.

Rawley Forbes heard it, though, and he jumped forward only to have her order him back. She stepped up into the carriage and said, "Oh, Rawley, I have done such a stupid thing. I lost my bag and my husband will be furious. I was supposed to pick up this dress for dinner tomorrow night. You know, I believe you've been invited too, and I have nothing to pay for it, not even a cheque. I am sure I could let them send Gerald the bill but then he would know. What shall I do?"

"Oh, I say, no problem at all. Here, let me."

"Oh, I couldn't. How will I repay you?"

"No need. A present. After all the trouble I caused you this afternoon, a peace offering. I say, do take it. Take what you need."

"You're a dear, a lifesaver. I could almost kiss you but considering what happened the last time and where we are I'll save it for a more private time and place." She flashed him her most vivacious smile and disappeared from view.

Rawley Forbes felt better already. Once he had solved the problem of the girl everything would be fine again.

CHAPTER TEN

Rawley Forbes was in a state of consternation. To begin with, he had gone to the huge party to which all the Forbes had been invited with the express purpose of seeing as much as possible (and seemly) of Sophia. Instead he had been given one meagre dance and the rest of the time she had assiduously avoided him. She was wearing a new gown on which she got many compliments (he supposed it was the one he had paid for) and she looked stunning. So stunning that he could hardly get near her and barely managed the one dance. Her husband was in attendance, but that, Rawley knew, was not the reason she ignored him. Other young men were dancing with her, drinking with her, taking her into supper. He was on the outside, being punished. And he had thought it was all over, her anger. He had done everything he could for her. Of course he had failed to get rid of Miss Linton, but Sophia could hardly know that. Besides, only slightly more than a day had passed. No, she was simply annoyed with him and he would have to wait until he got an opportunity to get back in her favor.

The Fitzhughs were there and Angelique danced often with Cedric who was only slightly better on the dance floor than he was in conversation. Still, he knew everyone, was accepted by everyone, so, Rawley could not help notice that his sister was being introduced to many important people whilst he was out in the cold. He was having a really miserable time. His cousin, James and his wife, Valerie, seemed to be enjoying themselves, but then James was now a part of the group, a "Sir."

When he danced with Angelique, she chided him. "Why so grim, Brother? You look as if the weight of the world were on your shoulders. Are you not enjoying yourself?"

"Not much, to tell the truth."

"You must never tell the truth. But why, pray tell?"

"I am bored. I hardly know anyone. I feel an outsider."

"Brother, we *are* outsiders, but not so much as before. And soon, well, I don't mind telling you that Cedric has been positively dashing, for him. Well, we shall see. But it takes time. What happened to your glamourous marquise? I should have thought she would have you . . ."

"Don't mention her."

"Have a tiff?"

"Not exactly. But, yes, she is a bit angry with me over something that . . . well, I cannot tell you. By the way, what do you think of Miss Linton?"

"Who?"

"The nursemaid to the brats."

"I don't, oh, Charlotte, yes. Miss Linton. From the country. She is most agreeable. Rather pleasant. Quite intelligent. Thinking of transferring your affections?"

He flushed with anger. "No! I don't like her, to be frank."

"Oh, well Lisette does. She confided as much to me. And she said that Juny does, too. Valerie is so pleased to have them off her hands and more or less behaving themselves that she wouldn't care if Miss Linton had two heads, which she doesn't, but one rather pretty one as a matter of fact, which is why I thought . . . you could do worse. She's not just a common servant, you know. But whether you like her or not, I suspect she is here to stay. So don't look so downcast. She won't bite you. I daresay she hardly notices you. . . . Ah, does the wind lie there? You *want* to be noticed."

"Not at all. I tell you I can't stand her. I was just curious about your reaction to her."

"I find her quite charming, Rawley. But do try to have a better time. Or at least look like you are having a better time. They'll think you don't approve or something. Talk to some of the young men. You know enough of them from your gaming. We've gotten ourselves invited to the big parties, but we must hope for invitations to the *intime* ones, too. And that won't happen if you go around looking like you are about to challenge someone to a duel."

"What do you mean?"

"You know perfectly well what I mean. Just mind your

manners and use good sense, Brother. I won't have my fortune spoiled by you."

After her admonition, he did try. He met a few friends, had a few drinks, danced a little, and seemed in general to disport himself in the proper mode, but his heart wasn't in it. When several of the gentlemen suggested going on to a gaming house, he excused himself, saying that he was feeling poorly. He left early, earlier than his sister or cousins and, dispirited, returned to Prospect Lane at about one o'clock in the morning.

He was surprised to find so much light in the house. Candles seemed to be glowing from almost every room. And when he came in the front door he was equally surprised to find several of the servants including the girl Beth and Kelsey, the major domo of the establishment, on the stairs, he on his way up, she on her way down.

He was so absorbed in his own thoughts that he hardly paid any attention other than to note that it was indeed odd for servants to be up and about this late at night. He nodded to Beth as she passed him on the stairs and then when he got to the top turned to the right to go down the corridor to his own room. As he did so he bumped into, of all people, his nemesis, Miss Charlotte Linton.

"Why don't you watch where you're . . ." He stopped short. There was concern on her countenance, and more than that, she, too was up and about. It came to him in a flash and would have come to him sooner had he not partaken of too much wine, someone was ill. "What's the matter?" he snapped, his words harsher than he meant them to be.

"It's Lisette, she has a high fever and stomach pains. She's been sick for several hours. We sent for a physician. He should be here soon. I also sent one of the servants around to inform Lady . . . your cousin. You probably passed one another on the way."

Suddenly he was quite sober. "Is it . . . serious?"

"I don't think so. Just a bad cold, I think. And croup. We all had it at home and the symptoms were the same. Once we get the fever down and she can sleep, she'll be all right. Nevertheless, to be on the safe side, I decided to send for the doctor and her mother. But there is nothing to worry about, beyond the normal worry one should have. Excuse me, please."

She tried to pass him, but he stopped her. "Look, can I do anything? Help in any way? Want me to go in and see her?"

"There is really nothing to do. I don't think she wants to see anyone right now except her mother. You might wait downstairs for the doctor and bring him right up to Lisette's room. No, wait, you could go and talk to James. He seems quite distressed."

"Is he . . . does he have it, too?"

"Not at the moment, but he's liable to get it. Once one child gets it, it seems to go around. Tell him not to worry."

Again she tried to pass him and this time he let her go, marveling at the way he allowed her to order him about, to tell him what to do. He called after her, "You might have sent for the surgeon sooner."

"I might have but she's only just taken a turn for the worse."

He mumbled something that she didn't quite understand and she went on to Lisette's room. He stood there for a moment and then decided that he really didn't want to talk to James, he just wanted to rest. Halfway to his room, he changed his mind. It might do some good and besides he hadn't really spoken to the boy since the incident the afternoon before. Best to find out how things stood.

He retraced his steps and went to James's room which was opposite Lisette's. He listened at her door for a moment but could hear nothing so he stepped across the hall and tapped lightly on James's door.

He thought he heard a weak, "Come in," and he pushed the door open. James was propped up in bed, a candle lit on the table beside him, thumbing nervously through an old book.

"Hello there, Jamie-boy. Bit lively around here, what?" He never quite knew how to speak to the boy so he affected a casual and mature air, and James, grateful that someone at least treated him like a grown-up, responded in kind.

"Yes, poor Lisette. She's got something dreadful. She's been heaving over there and Miss Linton says she has a high fever. They've sent for a doctor. You don't think it is serious, do you?"

"Sure it isn't. Just a cold and some croup, something

along that line. Remember having it meself. About her age—or yours. Nothing to worry about."

"Do you think I'll get it?"

"Shouldn't wonder. But, perhaps not. How do you feel?"

"Oh, fine. Except my ankle hurts. My arm is almost healed already."

"Your ankle?"

James looked chagrinned. "When I fell out of the tree yesterday."

"Hurt yourself, did you? Shouldn't wonder. Spying isn't done by a gentleman, Juny . . . eh, James."

"I wasn't spying, Rawley. Truly, I wasn't. It was just as Miss Linton tried to explain. We went to the park for a picnic. After we ate, someone, Lisette, perhaps, suggested a game of hide-and-seek. I didn't want to play. Children's game . . . but to be a sport, I agreed. Miss Linton was 'it' first, so I went down to the lake and climbed a tree, figuring she'd never find me there. That was when you and the lady came along in the punt. Then you got out. . . ."

"You should have announced yourself at once. Damned embarrassing."

"I should have only I didn't know but what you would be angry. I thought you would, well, kiss her and then go on, that sort of thing. But I wasn't spying. Then Miss Linton came up to you. She thought it was me and Beth and I fell out of the tree. I'm dreadfully sorry, Rawley. I won't say anything to anyone—ever."

"But you and Miss Linton discussed it, eh?"

"No. Only, we agreed never to mention it to a soul. She said something about as soon as it is forgotton . . . no, that's not it . . . the less you say, the sooner it is forgotton. But we really were not spying on you. We had no idea. . . ."

"All right, old chap. As you say, the less we talk about it, the better for all of us." He winked at James. "Pretty attractive lady, what? Between us men of the world."

"Oh, yes, devilishly attractive. Still . . ."

"Still . . . ?"

"I think Miss Linton is prettier."

"You do, eh. Well, she isn't. She couldn't hold a candle to So . . . to the other. Got a schoolboy crush on her, have you?"

"No! I just meant, she's been very decent."

"Seems to me she makes you toe the mark a bit."

"Well, I didn't like her at first, but look at the way she's taking care of Lisette. And she fixed up my ankle and she told me it would be all right . . . and well, just everything."

"All right. I can see that you like her. Call it what you like. She doesn't impress me much, though."

"You like the other lady, then?"

"Yes, I confess I do."

"What's her name?"

"That, my dear young chap, is a secret. Best for you not to know. Might be trouble if you did."

"Was she the one you were going to fight a duel over?"

"My, my, you have big ears as well as big eyes. Up in a tree listening to me talking to your father?"

"He was yelling rather loudly. I couldn't help but overhear."

"Didn't exactly hurry on your way, though, did you, when you heard him yelling?" Rawley was smiling, so feeling relieved, James nodded yes.

"Well, I didn't fight no duel, Jamie-boy. But if I was to fight a duel it would be over that lady, that's for sure. But you must never mention you saw us together. Some day, should you happen to meet her, you must pretend you never saw her before. That is what's expected of a gentleman. Give me your promise."

"My word, Rawley, I'd never. It was just what Miss Linton said, if we ever saw her we would act like we had never seen her."

"I can see Miss Linton has taken care of everything. But you just mind *me*, Jamie, and we'll be friends, we will. And maybe I'll bring you a present from up north."

"Up north?" James looked at him. "Are you planning a trip?"

"Later in the summer. I'm sure to be invited."

"Well, I may be going north too. Lisette and I. Miss Linton mentioned it this evening while we were eating. You had already gone to the party. She said she would ask Mother if Lisette and I could visit with her family in Suffolk. They have a big house, lots of land, and she has brothers and sisters. Her father will take me hunting and fishing, she said. Her uncle, too."

"Well, now I see why you like her so. And Lisette, does she want to go, too?"

"Yes, very much. There will be lots of girls near her own age. Let's see, there's . . ."

"Never mind, I don't need to know. You better go off to sleep now. Get some rest."

"I want to wait up for the doctor and Mother."

"Suit yourself. I'm going off to my bed, though. As soon as I'm sure your sister is fine," he added. He crossed to the door. "Remember, now, we have a secret. You never saw the lady before."

James put his hand over his heart. "Solemn oath," he said.

In the corridor Rawley stopped at Lisette's door. He could hear sounds from inside. Evidently the doctor had arrived while he was talking to James. He decided to wait and was rewarded moments later when Charlotte bustled out into the hall, again almost bumping into him.

He started to speak but she put her finger up to her lips. "The doctor is here and so is Lady Forbes. They arrived together about five minutes ago. He's given Lisette something to stop her sickness. Thank you for attending to James. Despite how he may have behaved, he was quite concerned and frightened."

"He didn't seem all that frightened to me. But how is Lisette?"

"She'll be fine. The doctor confirmed my opinion. A cold and croup."

"You are really quite remarkable, aren't you?"

"I beg your pardon."

"Correct diagnosis, confirmed by the surgeon. Complete understanding of James. Even had a talk with the lad, didn't you, about what you saw yesterday. Took care of everything for me."

"I really think that I should retire. I am quite fatigued and as your cousin and the doctor . . ."

"No, I think you should answer me."

"I didn't know you had asked a question. You made several statements and I don't choose to disagree with them."

"The little lass from the north country—full of home remedies for every occasion."

"Good-night, sir."

She started down the hall and he, angry that she would

not even argue with him, followed her. "I was going to have you discharged."

Charlotte shrugged. "If you mean," she said, as she continued to walk toward her room, which was in the opposite direction of his, "that you were planning to suggest to your cousin that I was spying, I doubt that you would have done so. If you were planning to ask for my discharge because you did not think me satisfactory for the children, then, of course, you would have been well within your rights to make such a suggestion to Lady Forbes. I would have told her that I thought I was not only qualified but that I was doing an exemplary job and fulfilling all of my duties. It would have been up to her to decide which of us was correct. This is my room, sir, and I am going inside and then retiring for the night. Good evening, sir."

He put his hand on the door. "Just a minute. You still have not answered my question. Why did you spy on me?"

"Please, sir, it is late and there is no need to go through all of this again. I told you then that I was not spying nor was James. Our meeting was quite coincidental. And I assure you I have already put the incident from my mind."

"Incident?"

"The meeting."

"You think less of me. You saw me embracing So . . . the lady. More North country judgment."

"I am not from the North country, sir. Suffolk is only a day's journey and a little more. We are country folk, it is true, but we are not a million miles from the hub of the universe. And I pass no judgment on you or the lady."

"But you think me ill-mannered, rude, a boor, a rake."

"Your words, sir. Not my own. An embrace between a gentleman and a lady is hardly boorish or ill-mannered if both are in accord. Even in Suffolk people embrace."

"I'm sure they do." He was losing at every turn, at every toss of the dice, and yet he couldn't stop. Some devil was in him. He told himself it was the champagne and the frustration of the evening. "But you think me rude."

"The only time I thought you rude, sir, was when you spoke rudely to me and accused me of something that I had not done. No, that is not quite so. On one other occasion, I also thought you rude."

"And when was that, pray tell?"

"On the occasion of our first meeting, sir."

"Our first meeting? I did no more than wish you a good day."

"That was our second meeting. The first was earlier in the day. When I was waiting in the rain at the hostelry for a hackney and you came out and took one that came along without asking me if I would like it or even if I would like to share it. No gentleman would have done that. Good-night."

He remembered it now, remembered her face. There was nothing more to say. Like a gambler who knows that his last throw will be his worst, yet compelled to do it, he took her in his arms and kissed her and then before she could struggle or cry out, released her.

She slapped his face and he said, "Well, at least I know that even in the North country or wherever, they are not always icy cold. Good-night to you, madam."

He walked away before she could answer. It was only the second time she had ever been kissed. She stood there in wonderment saying to herself, how dare he do such a thing? How dare he? Tears brimmed in her eyes as she went into her room and closed the door. But despite the salt of the tears she could still feel the taste of his mouth on hers.

CHAPTER ELEVEN

For the next few weeks the days passed quickly and uneventfully for Miss Linton; she was busy with the children and she hardly ever saw the adult Forbes except in passing, for they seemed to all have joined in the social whirl of London. She told herself it was just as well. She had a job to do, she enjoyed the children, and they had grown to like and, what was even more important, to respect her.

Then, one day, she received an invitation from Aunt Judith. It was a rather long note, asking her to come to dinner on the 27th and adding that Dunreath would be there, as well Uncle George and Jack. The Fitzhughs were coming, that is, Cedric and Lady Constance, and Aunt Judith had invited Sir James and Lady Forbes and their cousins, Angelique and Rawley as well. Finally, there would be a surprise for her, but Aunt Judith would not even hint as to what that surprise might be.

She desperately wanted to see Dunreath or else she might have tried to think of an excuse for not accepting. Jack Ellicott would be there and so would Rawley Forbes. One professed to love her and wanted to marry her; the other professed to loathe her and wanted her gone. It would not be an easy situation but, on the other hand, there was a large group. She mentally counted them, eleven not including the surprise, assuming the surprise to be a human being and not a present of some sort. The table was unbalanced, six women and five men. It was the kind of thing she would not have thought twice about in Suffolk, for at Linton Park, except on a rare formal occasion, the table was simply full of whomever happened to be present; but here in London much store was set by such things and she could not imagine her Aunt Judith making so obvious an error as having the women outnumber the men. By deduction, then, the surprise would be a man. But whom?

Well, it was only a week away, she could wait. In the meantime she would have to decide what to wear. Her formal gowns, although acceptable, were not the most chic. She didn't want to look a country bumpkin especially in front of Lady Constance, her father's elder sister, nor in front of Mr. Rawley Forbes, she admitted. He already thought of her as someone who worked in the fields stacking hay, or milking cows, and although it was true as a young girl she had learned to do such things, the Lintons were gentry and not peasants, a distinction he did not seem to grasp.

She dare not purchase something new, but she did decide with Beth's help to shop in one of the markets off the main thoroughfares where yard goods of excellent quality could be purchased. If she found what she wanted, Beth had agreed to help her make her own gown, for sewing was an accomplishment of both young ladies. Charlotte had grown very fond of Beth, partly because she was of an age to remind Charlotte of her sister Anne and cousin Dunreath, but also because the girl was good-hearted and helpful in so many ways. Charlotte decided that she would ask if Beth might accompany herself and the children on the trip to Linton Park. When she broached the subject with the girl (desiring her agreement before she asked Lady Forbes) she was delighted to find that Beth not only acquiesced but was grateful, too, for she had never been away from the city of London and she longed to see what places such as Suffolk were like.

But in the meantime there were the yard goods to be purchased, a pattern to be made, and the material to be cut and stitched. They would be busy, especially as both had full-time duties to attend to that could not be set aside for something so whimsical as a new gown.

They took the children shopping (after obtaining permission from Lady Forbes) and found in one of the by-ways of London a small shop that seemed to have only dry goods of excellent quality. And the prices were quite reasonable. They spent some time looking at the various materials, pleased by the large selection, before finally deciding on a lavender silk that was quite plain and would not be ostentatious. Beth suggested they get a few yards of tulle and use it to cover the bodice, for its web-like design would add a sparkle to the gown and still it would not be pretentious.

"Won't it take a lot of extra time?" Charlotte asked.

"Not too much. But if we are behind and can't do it, you can still wear the gown without the tulle and then add it on later. It will be like having a second gown." Charlotte immediately agreed and their purchases made, they left the shop with Lisette and James (he was none too happy in the store, but once they were outside he came to himself again) and decided to walk for a while and study the shop windows.

They made several turns and found themselves back in the fashionable section of the city, walking along the Strand toward Charing Cross, not too far from home. But as they had been on their feet for some time and had walked all the way from Prospect Lane, Lisette and then James began to complain about being tired. As Lisette had been recently ill and as James's foot had only completely healed a short time before, it was decided they would find a tea room in which to rest and refresh themselves.

They walked up Southhampton and then turned left into Maiden Lane where there were, Beth told them, numerous shops of the sort they sought. There were, indeed, several tea rooms, all rather sedate and decorous-looking, each one seemed from the cakes in its windows more inviting than the one before.

Finally they made a choice and went inside; they were not disappointed. The tea was hot and strong, the cakes moist and sweet. The children were delighted, and the atmosphere was pleasant and they so fatigued that they dawdled for more than an hour before Charlotte paid their bill and they left. Out on the street it had grown hot. They decided they would walk directly home, paralleling the Strand, along Maiden Lane into Charing Cross Road, across the Square (already named Trafalgar after Nelson's famous victory), and into Pall Mall, which would take them directly to Prospect Lane.

There were many fine shops to see and the heat was such that no one felt like hurrying. At the Haymarket on the far side of the Square they had to stop for a series of coaches were backed up and everyone was gaping. The reason was quickly obvious from the coat of arms on one of the most elegant carriages. The Regent himself was somewhere in the neighborhood, shopping no doubt, and everyone was anxious to see him and, if possible, be seen *by* him and perhaps even acknowledged.

The children wanted to wait and so did Beth; Charlotte was less enthusiastic, but she told herself that she had never seen the man, that he would someday be her sovereign, and that it would be an interesting tale to tell when she next wrote to Linton Park.

They waited for some time but evidently he was either in a shop or visiting someone for he did not appear. Slowly and reluctantly the crowd began to disperse, only those with absolutely nothing else to do, no work or business to get to, no pressing appointments, stood on, waiting and hoping for a glimpse of Prinny.

Finally, at Charlotte's insistence, they crossed the road, preparing to continue their journey. As they reached the other side, a door opened and from one of the shops a servant, laden with boxes, stepped precariously out into the flow of traffic. James, who was looking behind, still trying to catch a glimpse of the Prince, bumped into the man and the packages as well as the man were sent flying.

The man was not angry for he realized that it was as much his fault as James's, so they all began to pick up the packages and put them back in his arms when the shop door opened again and through it came the lady that Charlotte and James had seen with Rawley Forbes. She recognized them at once and stopped short. Charlotte did her best to pretend that she did not know who was standing there, but James, his mouth agape made it clear that he did.

The servant said, "Sorry, Marchioness, a small accident. No one's fault. I'll just take these to the carriage."

At that moment the shopkeeper stepped out to help her wealthy client to her carriage. "I hope everything is satisfactory, Madame Sophia. Should there be any problems, just call on us and we will make adjustment. And I am to post the bill to the Marquise of Kent-Chillingham, as before?"

The young woman snapped, "Yes. As before." She glared at James and then at Charlotte, then hurried to her carriage into which the servant had already piled the various boxes. He helped her in and she, keeping her back to them the whole time, told him to drive home quickly.

The shopowner smiled in a friendly fashion at Charlotte and then said, "Lovely lady. Her husband hates to pay the bills, but he always does." She smiled again, almost in a conspiratorial way and then went inside, closing the door behind her to keep out the heat, the dust, and presumably those patrons who could not afford her prices.

"Who was that beautiful lady?" Lisette asked. "She looked at you, Charlotte, as if she knew you."

"Yes, she was very comely," Beth said. "A marchioness."

"Marquise in France," Charlotte replied absently.

"What?" Beth asked.

"Nothing. Well, we should be getting along. It's getting late. And we're all tired."

They started out and James drifted back to her side. "That was she, wasn't it?"

"Sh! We don't really know. We're best off to forget it. It was a chance meeting. It won't happen again. I'm sure of it."

"Rawley likes her. Is she married? The lady said . . ."

"It would be better if you forgot it, James."

"Oh, very well. But it is jolly interesting, all the same. She's quite attractive, isn't she?"

"Yes, she is. Now, no more."

They continued for some way in silence; in fact, it wasn't until they had reached St. James Street where they were to turn into Prospect Lane, that he spoke again.

"She'll tell him, you know."

"Perhaps. But it was hardly our fault. Maybe she won't mention it."

"You mean because she's married. Poor Rawley."

"Yes, indeed. Poor Rawley."

"Poor Rawley what?" Lisette asked, skipping back to them.

"Nothing," James replied. "You're too young."

"All right, don't tell me. I shall ask him, why you and Miss Linton are feeling sorry for him."

"Don't you dare!" James shouted.

"It really isn't important, Lisette," Charlotte said quietly. "We were talking about how hard it is to get to know people in society. His sister you see, has been more successful, because she knows my Aunt and cousin. But we mustn't worry, Mr. Forbes will find his own way."

"He told me he may be invited hunting with the Prince," James said, seeing that Charlotte was trying to lead Lisette off on a tangent.

"There, you see. If that should happen, why he'll get to know all sorts of people."

"Will I?" Lisette asked.

"By the time you are old enough to go out in society, of course. And as James is going away to Harrow next year, he'll get to know ever so many people. And I know a few, in Suffolk, that I will introduce you to. In no time at all, you'll have many friends."

They had reached the house. When they went inside they found the servants bustling about, scrubbing and dusting and polishing. Kelsey spoke quietly to Beth who nodded, handed over the packages she was carrying and said that she had some work to do. Charlotte sent the children to their rooms and was preparing to go to her own when Kelsey said that Lady Forbes wished a word with her. Charlotte went straight to the drawing room and there she found her ladyship pondering a list.

"Ah, Charlotte, perhaps you can help me? Something has come up. My husband has sent a messenger from the city that he has invited a business acquaintance and his wife to dine with us this evening. Hardly enough warning, if you ask me, but we shall manage. I am trying to arrange a table. It is all very complicated. I thought it would be nice if we had at least one extra person and then, of course, that would make it uneven—here, let me explain. There will be the gentleman and his wife, my husband and myself, Rawley and Angelique. Naturally, I could ask you to eat with the children and I know you would not mind. . . ."

"Not at all."

"No, hear me out. But that makes it a rather uncomfortable six, conversation may not flow exactly as it should, and then I remembered that we had been meaning to ask Cedric Fitzhugh, your cousin, as he and Angelique are such friends. Well, I know it was rather late but I sent round to his house and I received a most gracious note in reply that he was, indeed, free this evening, and would be delighted to join us. Of course, that makes seven. So, in fact, I will expect you to eat with us after all."

"Of course, whatever you say. I am afraid I don't have anything to wear that would be totally appropriate. As a matter of fact I was out this very day shopping for . . ."

"Nonsense, you always look charming. I'm sure that your best country gown will be more than sufficient. It is after all just a small—I might say *intime* gathering— everyone will understand. Now say no more about it. I insist that you come. I am sure Rawley will be delighted to be seated with you and you know your cousin Cedric quite well, and Angelique and James and myself. You will not be ill-at-ease, I assure you."

"Well, of course, if you insist. Perhaps I had better retire and see to having a bath and finding the most appropriate dress."

"Yes, of course. Now, do not worry. You will look lovely. And I am sure you make small talk very well. Everyone will want to know about Suffolk from whence you come."

"Why is that, pray tell? There is little there that London folk would find interesting."

"No doubt that is true. But Prinny is organizing a shoot in that area next month. It plans to be quite a social event. Grouse or something. Whatever they hunt at this time of year. It will be an important event and all of the young men hope to be invited, all bachelors, I am told. Rawley will be most upset if he isn't . . . well, that is no matter. I am sure everyone will want to know all that you can possibly tell them about your native region."

"Very well, if they ask me, I'll do the best I can. Mostly I can say that it is beautiful and the people are kind and . . ."

"Yes, well, run along. Attend to your person. I have to see Kelsey about the menu. I'm sorry that you took Beth. . . ."

"But . . . I apologize . . . but . . ."

"No, no, it's all right. I gave you permission. I just hope that everything goes well. I do wish he had given me more notice. These are important people. They can be very . . . helpful. And James is contemplating a business deal of some sort. I don't really quite understand that sort of thing. So we will all be on our best behavior. Make sure the children are apprised of the fact that they are not to make an appearance. You have done wonders with them, Charlotte, in the few weeks you have been here, but I see no reason for them to be seen or heard."

"No, I will explain that they are to eat in the playroom and stay in their rooms for the evening. I'll give them some extra studying to do."

"Good idea. Now run along. And send Kelsey to me, please."

Charlotte did as she was bid, found the butler in the front hall and gave him Lady Forbes's message. He pursed his lips, nodded, said something to one of the girls and then hurried off. Charlotte had been about to ask him who the important guests were that had been invited at the last minute, but she did not have time.

When she got to her room she found the children waiting across the hall. She told them the news and gave them some work to do that evening, admonishing them along the way that they were to be quiet and not to come downstairs. Then she went down the back way to see the cook to tell her that the children would be fed upstairs. On the way up to her room, she met Beth.

"Isn't it exciting," Beth said. "And really such a coincidence."

"What do you mean? Coincidence?"

"Well, I think I'm right. When Juny ran into that man today, I believe I heard the fine woman who ran the shop say something about a Kent-Chillingham. That's who's coming to supper. The Marquis and Marchioness of Kent-Chillingham."

CHAPTER TWELVE

Charlotte was tempted to plead indisposition and ask that she be excused from attending Lady Forbes's dinner party. She didn't, of course, because she knew that Lady Forbes would be upset, that there would be an extra man, and that it would cause such confusion that she could not justify it in her own mind, especially considering the state that her employer was already in. Consternation was hardly the word. And although it would not be totally dissembling to say that she was indisposed (as soon as she heard who was coming, she felt ill) still it would not be fair. She would go and be polite and pretend never to have seen the lady in question before.

What, she wondered, was the Marchioness of Kent-Chillingham thinking at this moment? Had her husband told her earlier? She would not expect to see Charlotte. Surely she would be upset, too, would try to find an excuse not to come, but as it was now nearly five o'clock in the afternoon and the dinner party was scheduled for eight, it seemed unlikely.

And what would Rawley Forbes think when his cousin told him that they were having guests for dinner and who the guests were? And then, that Miss Charlotte Linton had been invited to make the table seating even? He would, she judged, be extremely concerned and do all in his power to change the arrangements.

Which was exactly what was happening below in Lady Forbes's writing room while Charlotte was upstairs having her bath.

Rawley was pacing the floor. The room was small, so his pacing, perforce, was limited; but nevertheless he paced. And as he paced, he pondered, trying to control his temper, for he did not wish it to become apparent to his cousin's wife that something was afoot.

"But, Val," he was saying, "such short notice. Couldn't you at least postponed it a day?"

Bitterly she answered, "I could have happily postponed it a week, but James did not consider that; the message was concise and clear. He was having two people to dinner. I was to make the arrangements, send off a formal note to the Marquise or Marchioness or whatever she is, the invitation would be expected and accepted. Evidently *her* husband sent her some message or other. No doubt she is as concerned as I. . . ."

"No doubt . . ." Rawley murmured.

"What? Never mind. I'm sure it made her change plans, rearrange her life. But at least she doesn't have to be hostess. She just has to appear."

"But couldn't it have just been the six of us? Or even just the four of you? Angelique and I could have found other things to do."

"A dinner party for four, all of them strangers? How grim. That's why it had to be more, but it would have been one-sided in a sense, four Forbes, two Kent-Chillinghams—what a ridiculous name, one can hardly pronounce it. I do hope I can find out her first name. . . ."

"Sophia."

"Oh. How do you know?"

"I've been introduced to her once."

"How nice. That will make it easier. Anyway, six seemed not quite right and then I thought of Cedric. It would impress him that we are entertaining titled people and I dropped him a note and to my surprise he accepted. That made seven. A bad number at table."

"But why Miss Linton? She's . . . she's so . . . provincial."

"Nonsense, you just haven't paid enough attention to her. She's quite clever. And you know, just because she is not London society doesn't mean that she isn't a lady. In fact she is well-connected, as you do know. She's Cedric's cousin, Lady Fitzhugh's niece. She's also a niece to the Ellicotts who have been most kind, and in fact . . ."

"Yes, I know all about her pedigree. She's not a show horse, after all. She's a servant in this house. You simply cannot invite a servant to dine with important people."

"She's more than a servant. And she has good credentials. The Kent-Chillinghams need not know that she is here to look after Lisette and James. She'll make a good appearance, she'll know how to handle herself. She has breeding, you know. I've watched her. In fact, dare I say this? To you, yes. I've hoped that her behavior would encourage us all. You, especially, Rawley, have not the proper . . ."

"What! You're going to tell me that a little thing from the provinces . . . I am a gentleman."

"Barely. And only through James's money and connections. The less said about our ancestry, the better, don't you think?"

"Surely you could have found someone else. . . ."

"At that late date? Hour? I hardly expected Cedric Fitzhugh, but fortunately he rose to the occasion. To send off to some woman I hardly know and ask her to come to dinner at the last minute, it would be most unseemly. I knew I could trust Cedric—he's rather gone on Angelique, I do believe. At least I hope so. He's so well-mannered, one can never tell what he is thinking, if one could understand him. Once he agreed, then Miss Linton seemed the right person. Now stop fretting. Everything will be fine. Besides, I must bathe and get dressed. Oh, I hope Kelsey and the cook have everything under control."

She got up and left the room, leaving Rawley pacing, wondering what he should do next. He was certain that Miss Linton would let it all out—no, she dare not. And if she was that well-bred . . . But what was Sophia going to think when she saw that face? What was she going to do? Rawley Forbes felt like killing himself. But only for a brief moment. Finally he shrugged. Whatever happened it would happen. Of course he should have tried to get rid of Miss Linton immediately after . . . but that was impossible. Besides, some time had passed. Perhaps Miss Linton would not even recognize Sophia. God, he hoped that would be the case!

At least the meal, the wine, the service were perfect. Had it not been for that, Lady Valerie Forbes might have considered the evening the worst night of her life. It was apparent at once that Sophia Kent-Chillingham would have rather been anywhere in the world, even the darkest depths of India, than at the Forbes home. Rawley was also distressed, only in a different way. He kept looking at Miss Linton as though she were about to do something horribly gauche, while the Marchioness looked at her not at all.

The gentlemen and Angelique paid no attention at all to what was going on and Miss Linton, demurely keeping her head down as much as possible, entered into the conversation only when she was asked a direct question. Then she was quite eloquent, for the questions had to do with (as Lady Forbes had predicted) the area around her home, Linton Park.

For the most part, though, the talk was mainly gossip and Charlotte, had she wanted to, would not have been able to join in, and so she listened, nodded her head sagely, added an appreciative sigh when she deemed it necessary, and waited until she was asked specific questions about Suffolk. The gentlemen especially wanted to know about it, although neither of the two that were married entertained great hope of being invited to become a member of the Regent's hunting party, as rumor had it that it was to be a bachelor affair.

"Well," she was saying in answer to a question from the Marquis, whom Sir James insisted on calling Gerald, and indeed they seemed quite chummy, "both my father and uncle hunt. That is, my uncle does and my father did. He rather gave it up except for rare occasions. He is an excellent shot. He tells a story of bagging thirteen grouse on his thirteenth birthday and promising never to grouse hunt again for he could envision the day when he would be expected to bag forty or fifty—in fact this year it would have to have been forty-five, I believe."

The gentlemen all laughed. Cedric Fitzhugh, stuttering as usual, but not in so pronounced a way, added, "I've h h hunted Linton lands. Charlotte and I are cousins, after all . . . and the area is very g g good." He paused a moment, took a sip of wine. "For grouse."

"Do you suppose the rumor is true," Angelique asked, "that it is to be a party of unmarried men only? After all the Regent is married."

"To his cousin," the Marquis said. "A state necessity, I deem it. If the ladies will excuse me, for all practical purposes he is a bachelor." There was a slight tittering before he went on. "For my part, I hope the rumor is not true. I should rather like to go. Don't hunt much, but when I do, I rather like it. How about you James?"

Sir James Forbes, who had never held a gun in his hand, answered, "Never has interested me much. Rawley, here, though, is quite a shot." That was not quite the case. Rawley Forbes had learned to shoot and considered himself somewhat better than he was, but his cousin had never seen him shoot. He was, in fact, only changing the area of interest away from his own deficiency. Rawley, who never minded a compliment, looked down modestly.

"I'm not really that good. I don't get enough practice. Still, I've hit a few in my day. Being a bachelor, I hope for the best. . . ."

What he didn't say was that if only bachelors were invited he might stand a better chance of receiving an invitation. He knew that James would do everything in his power to see that Rawley got that invitation. After all, James had been practically like a father to him, and when he had moved up in the world he had seen to it that Rawley and Angelique came along.

"Well, I am sure the ladies must be bored hearing about hunting. But tell us more, Miss Linton, about Suffolk." It was Sir James who asked. He had not traveled that much and he found that this was a good way to learn about places he had never been, to broaden himself by absorbing someone else's knowledge. He was pleased that his wife had thought of Miss Linton, who was quite attractive, and concise when asked a question. As a man who had made a lot of money quickly, he appreciated informed answers.

"Our land is quite beautiful and so is most of Suffolk. I really don't know it all. Just Linton Park and Dunreath Manor, that belongs to my Uncle George and Aunt Judith Ellicott, and the road between Bury and Newmarket. Of course, we have friends everywhere but mostly we stay at home or go to Dunreath Manor. It's very pretty," she added lamely.

"And what do you do, Miss, uh, Linton, is it? for a social life? In Suffolk?" It was the first time since they had been introduced that Sophia Kent-Chillingham had spoken directly to Charlotte.

"Well, we see each other a lot. That is, we visit one another's home and have dinners and parties and occasionally even a ball. Most of the families are rather large and are therefore self-contained. I, for instance, am one of eight children. I have an older brother and a younger one and five sisters younger than I. And I have cousins at Dunreath Manor, so there is never want of company. Then, too, we have things that we must do, even though the labor itself is done by locals, all of us have had chores to do since we were small children. We live a very full life, a busy day. And I might add, a contented one."

"Well said, young lady," Gerald Kent-Chillingham remarked. "I wish we in London could be more contented with what we have. Always traveling about, making calls, shopping, busy, busy all the time. No time for reflection, no chance to really appreciate nature."

"That might be all right for you, Gerald," his wife said, "but I've never noticed you appreciating nature. And no one is busier than yourself. You London men complain of your London wives but you leave us with so much free time on our hands, what are we to do but shop and visit and gossip? Pray answer me that."

"Oh, I have no doubt what you say is true, Sophia, but look where it leads, so many of our acquaintances, left to their own devices, feel it necessary to carry on an intrigue behind a husband's back. Usually nothing more than a silly flirtation, but we all know where that can lead. Ah, if it were only visiting and gossiping and shopping. . . ."

"Well, if certain women do such things, husband, I can only say that it is because they have been left to their own devices too long. They are bored. Don't you men understand that we women are bored by your continual talk of money, of making money."

"Except," Angelique said, breaking the tension, "when we go out to spend it."

Cedric laughed uproariously and the others, surprised by his reaction, joined in.

"Yes," Sir James said, "we all live rather splendidly."

"I, of course," Kent-Chillingham mentioned, "don't exactly have to go to trade to earn my money, but still it comes from trade and land. That is, from shares. And I must watch over my shares and see that they give me a decent return."

"I don't care about such things," Sophia complained. "If we must talk anything other than gossip, let us hear Miss Linton expound more on Suffolk and Newmarket and all those strange and exotic places. I vow, I wish someone here had been to Araby."

"My brother has been to Egypt," Charlotte said. "He is in the Royal Navy. An ensign. He's seen the pyramids and the like."

"Too bad he isn't here," Rawley drawled and again they all laughed.

She took it as a jibe at herself for talking too rhapsodically about her home, but yet she had done nothing more than answer their questions.

"But, Miss Linton," Sophia again queried, "does nothing ever happen in Suffolk? Nothing of interest, that is. Surely there must be choice tidbits about your neighbors?"

"I am sure that all sorts of things happen, just as they do in London, but we try not to talk too much about it in Suffolk. Besides, if I had any tales to tell they would be about people with whom you are not familiar and would thus not be interesting."

"Yes, that is true enough. Perhaps, though, in London you have seen . . ."

Rawley interrupted her. What was she trying to do? Bait Miss Linton into saying something? He could understand Sophia being angry, but what she was doing now was foolhardy. Her husband was present.

"Miss Linton does not get out much. She spends a great deal of time with Val's children."

Valerie, who was vaguely uneasy and realized that there was a charge in the air that could lead to trouble, but yet did not understand in the least why there should be ill-feelings between the Marchioness of Kent-Chillingham and Miss Charlotte Linton, added, "She has come to us as a great favor to work with Lisette and James. They are a bit behind in their schooling and Miss Linton has graciously come here at the request of Mrs. Ellicott. . . ."

"Oh, then you are an employee, Miss Linton. I apologize. I did not understand. I can see now why you have no time of your own to go about and learn the latest gossip. Close walks in the parks and on London streets are obviously not for you."

Completely oblivious, Valerie Forbes said, "Oh, not at all. Miss Linton only a few weeks ago had the children to St. James Park and this very day she went shopping. But I doubt she hears much gossip."

"But she may see things that are going on."

Charlotte looked away. "I nearly saw the Prince today. His carriage was nearby—Maiden Lane, I believe, and I was with the children. We waited but he did not appear."

"You did not miss much, my dear young lady," Gerald said. "He has grown rather obese. Sorry, James, I know you two are friends. Perhaps that is why he wants to go hunting. To get away from London."

"Oh, Lord, hunting again." Valerie Forbes stood up. "I believe we shall leave you gentlemen to your port. We shall be in the drawing room. Ladies."

The four women left. On their way into the drawing room, as the port and cigars were being passed, Rawley Forbes could hear Sophia Kent-Chillingham saying to Miss Linton, "I am sure you know much more than you say, Miss Linton. And I want you to tell me everything, especially about Mr. Rawley Forbes. He's devilishly handsome, don't you think? Or have you set your cap for him already?"

Rawley gulped down his port and bit on the end of his cigar. He would never understand women as long as he lived. It was obvious she was tormenting him, but why? Then it came to him in a flash. She was through with him. She dared take no more chances. Her husband probably knew everything. The Marquis had been eyeing him strangely for the past few minutes. Had she confessed all? Well, all wasn't so much. Still . . . damn women, he thought. Damn them all.

CHAPTER THIRTEEN

With Rawley and her husband not in the room, Sophia Kent-Chillingham no longer found it necessary to attack, however subtly, Charlotte. The four women chatted amiably until they were joined by the gentlemen. Then, mercifully, it seemed for everyone except perhaps Cedric Fitzhugh and Angelique Forbes, it was time for the guests to leave. Both Sir James and the Marquis Kent-Chillingham had ignored the others for the most of the evening and they, too, did not seem concerned that the evening end. Nevertheless it did, with a flurry of bows and curtsies, appreciative thanks, guarantees that they would all see each other soon again, and the like. Sophia quite pointedly said good-bye to Rawley Forbes in a way that had anyone been listening (no one was) would have told said listener that this was not an ordinary farewell. He looked miserable. He was controlling his anger at both Valerie Forbes and Miss Linton. Together they had, however inadvertantly, conspired to break up what he had considered a budding romance, one that would have led him into the best houses in London on the arm of Sophia Kent-Chillingham. But the proximity had been too much for her. If only Miss Linton had not . . . Yes, it was all her fault. Even without the invitation from Valerie, Sophia was not one to take chances. Did her husband know that he had paid for that dress? Rawley wondered. Was that the reason? No, it was merely the ubiquitous presence of Miss Charlotte Linton from Suffolk. It was insufferable. And yet he would have to live with it. At least they had gotten through the evening without an incident, even though it seemed that Sohpia was determined to provoke one. As soon as the guests were

101

gone, barely muttering a good-night, he stamped off to bed.

Everyone was tired and soon followed him, although with somewhat more grace. If his bad humor was noticed, no one commented on it. Charlotte could see that he was angry, but she had determined to put it out of her mind. There was no reason for him to blame her for anything that had happened. She was going to ignore him, see as little of him as possible in the next few weeks, and then there would be the trip home. Only one event stood in her way, Aunt Judith's dinner the next week in which all the Forbes were included as well as Cedric and Lady Constance. Of course Dunreath would be there and that was something to look forward to. And Uncle George. But then, so would Jack. As she undressed, she teasingly thought to herself, perhaps Mr. Rawley Forbes and Jack Ellicott will become great friends that evening and therefore neither of them will pay any attention to me. She was curious, too, about the surprise guest. But that could wait. Now all she wanted to do was go to sleep. The wine, although she had drunk far less than anyone at the table, had made her drowsy.

She slept fitfully and was not feeling her best the next morning, but nevertheless she was up early (for both Lisette and James were early risers) and in the dining room when they trooped in for their breakfast.

Of course they wanted to know everything that had happened and she was hard-pressed to explain that actually nothing had happened, that when grown-ups had a meal together, whether it was called a dinner party or not, usually it was just an evening of conversation. No games, such as those played at children's parties, took place. Just conversation, she repeated to herself, aware that, indeed, a certain type of game had been played.

James finally got her alone and asked if the lady (for he had heard through the servant grapevine who the guests were to be) had recognized Charlotte and had there been any unpleasantness. Charlotte replied that she was sure that the lady had recognized her, but nothing untoward had happened, that from now on they would not discuss the subject and that she suggested, as Rawley Forbes seemed a bit out of humour, that it might be wise for James to absent himself from his older cousin's presence for the time being.

Then she sent him off to join his sister. There was work that had to be done each morning. After they had studied for a while by themselves, Charlotte invariably joined them. But thirty minutes or so of study alone gave them a chance to calm themselves and get in the right frame of mind for the few simple lessons she gave them each day.

She was about to leave, having finished her light breakfast, when Sir James Forbes, attired for the day, ready, she was sure, to go off to the city, came into the room. Before she could excuse herself, he said, "Sit down, please, Miss Linton. I'd like a word with you." Then he softened his voice, for the tone had been inperious, and added. "We've not had a proper chat since you joined us. My fault, I dare say. But, if you don't mind, we'll rectify that right now. Valerie is indisposed. Won't be down. Angelique sleeps half the day away—and I should imagine it will also be some time until we see young Rawley, for I noticed he had a rather heavy hand with the port last evening. Holds it well, though, I'll give him that. Sit. Sit. Just let me fill me plate," he was on his way to the sideboard, "and then we'll have that little conversation that is so long overdue."

He was back to the table in a matter of moments, his plate filled to the brim. He sat down directly opposite her and started to eat, not in a hurried fashion, but as one who has a chore one wants to complete and yet relishes doing, so that each bite seemed to please him not so much for its taste but for the fact that it moved him inexorably forward toward the end he expected to accomplish.

Carefully chewing each bite, he would swallow, look at her and than take another piece. In this way he had nearly emptied his plate before he finally spoke. "Take Rawley, for instance," he said, as though in the middle of a conversation. "What do you think of him? My wife, I daresay, has told you nothing much about us, has she?"

His eyes, which were blue, held her gaze in his. She had hardly noticed him before, but now she realized that he had a strong face, a determined one. There were flecks of gray in his hair, but he still looked young. When she didn't answer at once he said, "Take your time. That's two questions. I'll answer the second one for you. She didn't. Didn't say much at all. Can't say that I blame her. Well, what about Rawley? What's your impression?"

She felt trapped. Should she say what she felt or should

103

she temper her remarks. What exactly did he expect of her?

"That's all right. Say what you think. I can see you're thinking it over. Say what you think straight out, that's what I tell everyone who works for me. No use fibbing. I'd rather hear the truth. If you think I'm a fool, tell me so. That's what I say to them. They won't, of course. Too afraid they'll lose their position. I can tell, though. You don't like him, do you? Go ahead, I promise you won't lose anything for being honest. But I daresay I'm not the first to tell you that. Looks like you've got common sense."

"No. My father has told me the same thing many times."

"Well, then, out with it. I won't bite you for what you think. I've got a reason, young lady, I'm not just gabbin' and gossipin' like some London dandy."

She decided she rather liked him, more than she expected she would. He was a little rough, a little coarse almost, but not unlike older men she knew in Bury St. Edmonds and Newmarket and some of the ones that lived even closer to Linton Park.

"Well, he seems . . . in a hurry. He's rather full of himself, too. But he's not a bad person. I think he sometimes doesn't quite know why he does things. He wants to impress people. I can't say much more, because I really don't know the gentleman."

"You know a little more about him than you let on, but that's neither here nor there. You're right about him. He's really a good sort but he has some big ideas. All of them have. That's my fault. I tried hard to get where I am and I guess making it important for me, made it important for them. You see, Valerie and I sort of raised Rawley and Angelique in a way. We took them over when Lisette was a brand-new baby, that was nine years ago. He was ten, Rawley was, and Angelique, well she was a year or two younger. She's your age, I'd say, or a bit older. We had to, you see. Their mum and . . . well, there was a bad accident, a fire and they both died. They're not really my cousins, you see. We gave them our name . . . had to, they were nothing much, and it was easier. Well, that's family history and I know you'll never tell a soul. But Rawley, he has ideas about his station, in a way. I mean, I want him to do well, marry well, be accepted, be part of the gentry, but a lot of them are fools. Not all, mind you. Kent-Chillingham, isn't. Though, his wife . . . well, Rawley needs to do something. I gave him too much, both of them. Felt sorry for them, I did. And so they've grown up expecting a lot. Now Angelique, she's a nice girl and if your cousin *should* marry her, that would be fine—but I'm not counting on it and neither should she. She'd be a good wife for him, but if it isn't him, it'll be another. I just want her to be happy. As for Rawley, look, I'm going to lay it straight to you Miss Linton. My wife is a social climber. My fault, because I did a bit myself. But only in a business way. I never pushed for that garter. She's different. She wants everything and she's determined to get it. Now, I don't mind if she gets it fair and square and so long as she doesn't get hurt.

"Rawley wants it, too. But he hasn't been completely on the up and up. He tries to act like these young rakes and he really isn't their sort. He needs something else. Needs to settle down. Needs to marry the right girl. I'd be obliged if you'd—well, show him the way, help him to see that there's other things in life. You may even know some girls up there in Suffolk, that's what he needs. I know you have your hands full with my two and I appreciate what you've done, so does Val, and you can hardly take on a lout of a lad bigger and older than you as a pupil. Besides he'd have none of it. Not if he was to know. But if you could help him just by being yourself, being a lady . . . There's real worth in him but it needs bringing out. Am I clear?"

"What you say is clear enough, Sir James, but I'm afraid there is little I can do. Mr. Forbes and I are not exactly friends. Something happened. Well, it would be improper to repeat it. It is his secret and since then we have hardly spoken."

"I know, he can be a frightful snob. Don't know why. Nothing to be a snob about. But then, they're usually the worst, aren't they? Still, if you were to be pleasant with him, understand him a little, win him around, he might just listen to you."

"I doubt that."

"It's worth a try. I'd make it worth your while."

"It's not the money. . . ."

"I know. But try, anyway. I think you deserve more wages than what we agreed on initially. That'll start next month. No matter what you do. But make friends with him. You might do it through his sister. You have an opening you see. Your cousin . . . his sister . . . maybe somehow . . . I'd be obliged. He's got to come to work for me soon, at the end of the summer. He knows that. And he doesn't like it. Likes spending my money all right, but he . . . Well, just do the best you can and I'll be beholden to you. You won't be sorry you tried.

"There now, that's more than I've said at one sitting in all my life. You know more about us than most—which proves I trust you. I can see you're an honest girl. I'm trusting you with some secrets, but I'm a good judge of character. You take Prinny, for instance. Yes, I can call him that now. Well, he'll never repay that loan to me, I knew it when I gave him the money. That's why I got the 'Sir' in front of my name. Expensive little word. I won't tell you how much but that's all right. It was an investment and it paid off. I've got me a partner now, the Marquis of Kent-Chillingham. I'm handling his money and the two of us will make a lot. A year ago I couldn't have approached him; last month, he did me. Another secret. But do what you can for Rawley. Say you will."

"I will do what I can but I can't promise anything."

"I know, I know. So long as you try. I'll help any way I can, and I can in small ways. You'll see. He's not a bad sort. Nor am I. For all my rough edges."

Charlotte said, "I think you're a very good sort—and I think you and my father would get along very well."

"I'd like to meet the gentleman."

"Perhaps, if you come north you shall."

"We'll see. Well, I'm off. I get started early. Beat the other fellows out by getting in early, knowing what's happening before they awake. Like young Rawley there. You won't forget your promise."

"I won't forget and I'll try to be friends and set a good example."

"As much as I could ask for, at first." He stood up abruptly, gave a jerky little bow and said, "Good morning."

"Good morning to you, Sir James." When she called him that, he turned and winked at her and then scampered from the room.

Now, she thought, just what does this entail? I suppose nothing more than trying to be polite to Mr. Forbes, to show him by example, to show him . . . what? A thought was about to form in her head, a thought that she was somehow being used, that Sir James was not quite so open as he seemed, when she was interrupted by, most surprising to her, the very subject of her most recent conversation.

He looked not in the least as if he had not enough sleep or had partaken of too much port, but, on the contrary, the epitome of good health and spirits. That is his spirits seemed high (he was actually whistling when he came into the room) until he saw that she was present.

"Miss Linton," he said perfunctorily, "good morning."

"Good morning, sir."

We went to the sideboard, filled a plate (not so full as Sir James had) and then went to the far end of the table, quite obviously intending to ignore her.

She had finished her own meal, had nothing to say to him, and despite the admonishment of Sir James Forbes, saw little that could be done constructively at the moment, so she stood up, preparatory to leaving the room.

"One moment, please," he said, without looking up.

"Sir?"

"It may interest you to know that at least partially because of your interference I suspect I am no longer welcome in the Marchioness of Kent-Chillingham's home—or circle. You could easily have absented yourself last evening and she might have forgiven the error. You have made an enemy, Miss Linton, one who will never forgive you."

"You, sir or the Marchioness?"

"She would not deign to think of you again, I am sure. But I warn you, Miss, I wish you far away from me and all of my dealings. I cannot persuade my cousin to send you away. You have cleverly wormed your way in here, using the children and whatever wiles you possess, but I do not want again to find you involved in my private life nor that of my sister."

"Your sister?"

"Yes, Angelique. It is her opinion and mine that your cousin is considering a proposal. Should you do anything, anything to attempt to dissuade him, I will not be responsible."

"This is a message from you—or your sister."

"Angelique is not aware of your meddling nature. But we must protect one another. She is a good-natured person and would not see to what deviousness you can stoop."

Charlotte had never done anything like this before in her life. But suddenly she could not contain herself. All the words of Sir James came flooding back to her. All his requests for her to help Rawley Forbes, all his pleas that Rawley Forbes was really a good sort, that he merely needed to be set off in a different direction. And she, like a fool, had briefly—very briefly, it was true—thought such a thing possible. But now she could not control herself. His accusations were ridiculous in the extreme, as ridiculous as they were insulting.

"Mr. Forbes, it will give me the greatest pleasure never to speak to you again, sir. I assure you I care not about your private life, nor do I advise my cousin about his. But I am not used to being spoken to in the way that you have just done nor am I used to having certain other liberties taken. I am not so defenseless as you may think. I do not give warnings as you do. Suffice it to say that I believe you are no gentleman and in addition are behaving in as stupid and foolhardy a fashion as any person I have ever met. I will not interfere in your life, sir. And do you not interfere in mine! Or there will be the devil to pay!"

CHAPTER FOURTEEN

In every way, the dinner given by Aunt Judith was the opposite of that one given by Lady Forbes. Not only was Charlotte looking forward to it and to wearing her new gown that she and Beth finished only hours before it was time to dress, but the surprise that she had been promised turned out to be an extremely happy one. Even knowing that Jack would be there and so would Rawley Forbes did not dampen her enthusiasm as she prepared to leave for Aunt Judith's house in Mayfair. Because she would be seeing Dunreath and hopefully Dunreath would be well again.

It was going to be a perfect evening or as near perfect as she could imagine. And then, only a few days later, she would be leaving for Linton Park and taking James and Lisette with her for a fortnight's visit to her family. She had been gone from them less than two months and yet it seemed forever. For one thing, she told herself, it was because she had never been away from them all before. And for another, in truth, although she hated to admit it, she was already wearied of London. Too many things had happened, too many untoward, unexpected, and unfortunate things had happened that had marred her appreciation of the city.

But all of those thoughts were put aside in the excitement of the new dress, which she had to admit (agreeing with Beth) was lovely and which she knew (although she would not agree with Beth) would look lovely on her person. It was going to be a bonny evening. Nothing could happen, she would let nothing happen, to spoil it.

They took only one carriage, for there were just five of them leaving from the Forbes home on Prospect Lane. It was a slightly tight squeeze for all of them were dressed appropriately and the ladies gowns especially took up considerable space—for although they were not cut as fully as had been the fashion, still none of them had skimped on material. Then, too, the men were now wearing the longer coats with trousers and the coats were of a heavy cloth and cut fully to emphasize the men's shoulders.

Charlotte and Angelique sat on one side with Rawley between them while Sir James and Lady Forbes sat opposite them. The coach jostled them on the cobblestones and each of them was silent, trying as best he or she could to keep from being pushed up against the other. Fortunately the trip was only of a few minutes duration. When they arrived at the Ellicott house in Mayfair they could see all the candles ablaze. Several coaches stood nearby, but the Fitzhugh crest was not on either of them.

Relieved to get out of the carriage, Charlotte allowed Sir James to take her arm and help her down while Rawley looked the other way. Sir James then helped down Angelique and finally his wife and the five of them, guided by torchs held by the servants, went up the broad brick steps to Aunt Judith's lovely home.

Uncle George was there to greet them and Charlotte flew into his arms, then to her Aunt, and, standing behind her, Dunreath who, although she looked pale by the candlelight, seemed to be of a fuller face than when Charlotte left Suffolk. Jack, looking serious, was behind Dunreath and he shook Charlotte's hand as introductions were being made in the great front hall. In the shadow she could see a dark coat and then Jack stepped aside and the dark coat came forward, materialized as an ensign's uniform, and, in it, her brother, Arthur! The surprise guest.

It was almost too good to be true, her happiness, for the moment, was complete. There was a flurry more of introductions and then everyone settled down in the comfortable drawing room for sherry and conversation before dinner was announced.

They all were admiring a picture that hung over the fireplace. It was by, Aunt Judith explained, a little recognized friend of theirs, a landscape painter named John Constable, and the picture depicted rather accurately a pastoral scene reminiscent of their own Suffolk countryside.

"I would have invited John," Aunt Judith was saying,

"except that he is out of the city. In fact, he is seldom in London, which is perhaps why he is so little known or respected. Oddly enough, he tells me his paintings sell better abroad than they do here. I can not understand it. I like his work very much."

"Well, I am no expert, Mrs. Ellicott," Sir James said, "but I know what I like and if your Mr. Constable will come see me, I'll be happy to purchase one of his paintings if it is anything at all of the quality of that one there."

"How kind of you. I shall send him to you as soon as I hear from him. Ah, I hear a carriage. It must be Lady Fitzhugh and Cedric. Do you wish to hide again, Arthur?"

"I think not, Aunt Judith. No need to surprise Aunt Constance in the same way I did Charlotte. I don't think she would be particularly pleased."

"No doubt, my boy," Uncle George said. "She's a bit stiff," he added for the benefit of the Forbes clan. "But not as difficult as she first seems."

On Cedric's arm, Lady Constance Fitzhugh made a calculated grand entrance. She was bedecked in diamonds which were all the more striking because she wore a relatively simple, albeit old-fashioned, gown of dark burgundy. Lady Constance was not yet fifty, yet her hair was white and she walked so slowly and regally that if one did not know, one might have taken her for at least ten years her senior. And, if one did not also know, one might certainly have taken her for the Queen mother, if such a lady had existed. One knew one was in the presence of someone special when one saw Lady Constance. She looked, acted, and felt regal. It would have been hard not to have been awed by her at least a little, and the Forbes's were not the sort to be unimpressed under any circumstances.

The introductions took some time for Lady Constance also affected to be slightly hard of hearing (in fact, she never missed a syllable), and that made it necessary to speak slowly and even to repeat names. She greeted Charlotte and Arthur as she always had, slightly disdainfully allowing them to peck her cheek; then she offered the same privilege to Jack and Dunreath, although they were not blood kin, and finally she graciously accepted the bows, curtsys, and general felicitations of Sir James and Lady Forbes as well as Angelique, and Rawley, who was the last to be introduced.

She looked him over for a moment through her lorgnette, then nodded not quite in approval and said, "I have heard your name spoken. I do not recall, nor is it important, what the incident was, but I strongly suspect that it was something one prefers not to hear. I hope it shall not happen again."

Then she allowed herself to be seated in the best chair and by doing so instantly became, as was her wish, the center of attention.

After the general amenities had been taken care of, Lady Fitzhugh turned to Charlotte and said in a loud voice, "Tell me, Charlotte, what exactly are you doing? I am given to understand from Cedric that you are a governess of small children. Indeed, now that I think on it, the name is the same. Ah, now I understand. I believe I do. Judith, did you arrange all of this?"

"I did, Lady Constance."

"Well, I was about to comment disparagingly, but now I don't believe I shall. In truth, getting you away from that brood and into society is not such a bad thing, Charlotte. I trust your mother and father are well," she added as an afterthought.

"Yes, I believe so. I had a letter only yesterday and Dunreath saw them two days ago."

"Yes, Dunreath. How are you, child?"

"Feeling much better, Lady Constance."

"Good. You should stay in the country, though. London is a poor place for those with weak dispositions. Charlotte needs the city life for a while. And Arthur, you have been well serving His Majesty."

"Yes, sea life agrees with me, Aunt. Surprisingly."

"Not surprising at all. I had an uncle who went to sea. And it seems to me that two centuries ago there was a Fitzhugh who was a pirate." She laughed and the others joined in lightly.

Turning to Sir James, she said, "You will find in all the oldest families a pirate or two, Sir. That's how family fortunes get started. In a few generations everyone forgets and then we are treated as though the good Lord handed the money down directly to us, much like giving the tablets to Moses. You have a daughter, Sir."

"Lisette."

"No. That is not her name. It's French, but that's not it."

112

"Angelique . . . ?"

"Yes, she is the one."

"My niece."

"Ah, yes. Cedric has brought her to visit." She looked across the room. "You are the same girl?"

"I am Angelique Forbes, yes."

"Come closer, child. Let me look at you. Don't look much like your cousin, or is it in the female line?"

Sir James quickly said, "No, *my* cousin. Rawley there and Angelique are *my* cousins."

"Yes, well, he doesn't look like you either. In my family, well, Charlotte's father and I bear a striking resemblance. And Cedric and I look a bit alike. And when Cedric is with the Lintons he looks like he belongs there."

Charlotte said, "Dunreath and I, except for our coloring, have much in common."

"Yes," Lady Constance went on, "it is easier when families resemble one another. Less confusion, I believe. So tell me, Judith, how did you get George to come to this den of iniquity, London?"

"I told him he had to come in order to dine with you."

"Not that I believe you for an instant, but thank you for the compliment. Cedric, why are you not talking? I am being forced to keep the small talk alive. Do say something outrageously witty or clever. He can, you know, but he never does. Except when we are alone. I believe he is afraid he will hurt someone's feelings. I, on the other hand, often say . . . well, speak up, Ceddy. Does not Charlotte look most comely?"

"All of the ladies look ex . . . ex . . . exquisite, Mama."

"Brilliant. Witty. Clever. What did I tell you." Cedric laughed heartily and they all joined in.

Dinner was announced and Charlotte found herself being taken in by Rawley Forbes. The table arrangement was: George Ellicott and Lady Fitzhugh; Sir James took in Aunt Judith; Arthur was paired with Lady Forbes; Jack with Angelique; Cedric Fitzhugh with Dunreath; and that left Rawley for Charlotte, an arrangement that did not make either of them overly happy.

Nevertheless, the dinner was a success and the conversation kept moving at such a fast pace that Charlotte hardly had time to notice Mr. Forbes and he, although unfailingly polite, spent as much time talking to the lady on the other side of him, Dunreath, and the people across the table as he did engaging Miss Linton in conversation. What Charlotte longed for most was some time alone with Dunreath. What made her most uneasy was not the presence of Mr. Forbes, but of Jack Ellicott who continually looked across at her as though to suggest that he wanted to be alone with her. It had been so long ago, her birthday, that she could hardly remember it, except for Jack's insistence that they go off by themselves. She would not let that happen again.

Finally, after a long and tasty meal, Aunt Judith stood up and the other ladies followed her into the drawing room where they could talk while the men had their port, cigars, and a different sort of conversation. Charlotte immediately sought out Dunreath and the two girls sat side by side on a small sofa. They could not be rude and ignore the others, but they would be able to talk a little between themselves, exchange a few confidences, and make arrangements to meet soon when they might be alone.

Meanwhile, in the dining room, several decanters of port were being passed around the table and the gentlemen were lighting fine cigars imported from the New World. George Ellicott held the floor.

"I understand the Regent is coming North to hunt with a party of gentlemen. Do any of you know any more about it than that?" He looked around. "Is Suffolk his destination?"

Cedric said, "I . . . I believe so."

"A large party?"

"Ve . . . very. It was sup sup . . . supposed to b . . . b be bachelors, bu . . . but it isn't."

Sir James asked, "Have there been invitations sent?"

"Not . . . not . . . not that I kn . . . kn . . . know of."

"Do you hunt, Mr. Forbes?" Jack Ellicott asked Rawley.

"Yes. Don't know if I'll be invited, though." He seemed rather downcast.

"Don't know that any of us shall," Sir James said. "No great disgrace I should say, not to be included. All the rakes and wastrels he keeps around him. That Brummell fellow."

"Still I should like to go," Rawley said wistfully.

Sir James turned to Arthur, "I believe your sister is

bringing my two offspring for a visit to your home. Linton Park, isn't it?"

"Yes, Sir."

"Well, they're not the best behaved in the world. Tell your mother and father not to go too easy on them."

"When is she leaving, Charlotte and the children?" Jack asked.

"Damned if I know. Next week sometime."

"That's when Prinny leaves, too," Rawley Forbes said.

"Where will he be staying?" George Ellicott asked. "I'm not all that interested in royalty, you know, but if he's going to be in our bailiwick, we should know. I suppose we'll have to do something, damned if I want the whole crew at Dunreath Manor, though. A day's hunt, dinner, that sort of thing would be fine, but we'd not be able to put them up and neither would Henry, eh Arthur? That's Henry Linton, my sister's husband. Charlotte and Arthur here, their father. Linton Park is a big place, so is Dunreath Manor for that matter, but it would be quite an imposition."

"I believe," Sir James said, "that he spoke of renting a place. Probably not far from you, but a place that is empty at the moment."

"Wonder if he means old Boomer's place. Been closed up for several years. A few servants about, they keep the hay mown and air the place out. Big enough, twenty miles or so from us. Yes, that might be the ticket. Well, that's good news. Afraid I was going to have all sorts descend on me."

"Won't you be in London, Sir," Rawley Forbes asked. "I understand you just arrived. . . ."

"And going back as soon as possible. Brought Jack here and Dunreath down for a visit, but I'm going back, so is Dunreath, I think. Jack hasn't said. He has interests in town, but now . . ."

"I shall be going back, too. Next week."

Rawley Forbes looked at Jack Ellicott. It was clear Mr. George Ellicott had meant romantic interests and if his son had decided to go back then that was probably because of Miss Charlotte Linton. He felt a pang of annoyance which he certainly did not attribute to jealousy.

He said, "If I am invited, I hope that I may at least call

and pay my respects to you, Mr. Ellicott and your family. I assure you I won't bring the whole of the Prinny's hunters along. None of your so-called London rakes."

"By all means, my boy. I didn't mean to suggest that you, anymore than Cedric here, who will certainly be called, are like the rest of them. And I'll tell you what. If you aren't invited, don't take it to heart. Come along with Sir James's young ones. You're a cousin, right? Come along and stay with us. You'll be more than welcome, won't he, Jack."

"Oh, indeed, he will." But Jack Ellicott, too, had sensed something. Mr. Forbes had been around Charlotte for some time. He had taken her in to dinner. And he had been very anxious for an invitation to the hunt. His father might welcome him to Dunreath Manor, but Jack was not so sure that he really wanted to see Mr. Rawley Forbes in Suffolk, no matter what the circumstances.

CHAPTER FIFTEEN

Home! Back to Linton Park. Charlotte could not believe it, she was on her way home. How she had missed it, missed her mother and father, her sisters and brother, and now she was going to see them all within the hour. She could hardly contain herself. Even the children, Lisette and James, could tell that she was anxious. They had even commented on it.

The three of them, plus three passengers for Bury St. Edmonds, were speeding (insofar as the coach could speed over the rather rough Suffolk road between Newmarket, the busy town they had just passed through on their way from London, and home, that is, Linton Park) at a pace that jostled and jolted them all from side to side. Charlotte was in the middle between the two children and the three gentlemen, commercial travelers, sat opposite them. Soon the coach would slow down, for there were hills to be climbed, and then it would stop only two miles from the entrance to Linton Park where William Clapp the one-legged stableman would be waiting with a wagon to drive them and their belongings the rest of the journey.

The trip had been uneventful and for her tedious, but the children had enjoyed it enormously for they had never really been away from London and every step of the way made their trip an even greater adventure. Naturally they were a little uneasy about what they might find in the country (they somehow expected it to be primitive), but still they were overjoyed to be away from the confines of the Prospect Lane house and their mother. And, although they had certain trepidations, they were rather looking forward to making friends with children near to their own ages.

Charlotte, trying to make the time pass more quickly for herself and trying equally not to disclose her ever-growing anxiety, closed her eyes as though she were asleep (which she definitely wasn't, for sleep certainly would not come in her present state of anticipation) and attempted to review the events of the past few months, since her birthday, to put them in some sort of perspective. It was the last event of any note, Aunt Judith's dinner, that she thought of first.

When the gentlemen finally joined the ladies she had had little time to speak with Dunreath for, as usual, Lady Fitzhugh had dominated the conversation and politeness required that one pay her full attention all the time. But Charlotte and Dunreath had agreed to meet the next morning at Prospect Lane where, when the children were settled, they could talk. In the afternoon Dunreath was seeing Arthur and he would, she was sure, arrange to meet her at the Forbes household.

Jack Ellicott managed to stand beside Charlotte when the full group was gathered and he asked if he might see her the next morning. She explained that she was seeing his sister and that, unfortunately, she had her charges to see to, so that she would have little free time to give him while he was in London. He suggested that she was avoiding him, but he did it in such a nice way, and in such a rather dispirited fashion, that she felt guilt.

"I could," she said, "ask for the following evening off. Perhaps Arthur, Dunreath, you, and I might do something together? If that is convenient?"

"Jolly convenient. I'll arrange everything. We shall dine at the best restaurant in London."

"Now don't spend all of your Suffolk money on an extravagant meal."

"Leave it to me," he said.

And so, the four of them went to dinner together. It was a pleasant evening and Jack did not press her, nor did he comment at all on his private thoughts about the person of Mr. Rawley Forbes. That same gentleman had, inadvertantly (no doubt through the children) discovered that she was dining out and had made a snide comment to her about it whilst at the same time feigning indifference. She did not know what was the matter with him, but she ignored his comment. He, too, did not know quite why he should have bothered to care enough to even speak with her, but on the very same evening he went to a gaming house, drank too much, and lost a considerable sum of money.

The next morning his spirits were low until he received an invitation, written in the hand of the Regent's private secretary, asking him to join a party of gentlemen for a hunt in the Suffolk area two weeks hence. Temporarily, at least, he forgot his losses, forgot that he had too much to drink, and even forgot Miss Charlotte Linton, who seemed ever to be on his mind.

Charlotte learned most of this, too, from the children. That is, she learned of his invitation, learned that he had heavy losses at chemmy, and that he had drunk too much on the very night she was dining with her brother, Dunreath, and Jack. In truth she thought little of it, except to note that Mr. Forbes would no doubt be seen at Linton Park or Dunreath Manor sometime during her visit home. But she told herself that he was the least and last of her worries. Jack Ellicott, although behaving perfectly, had insisted that they have a long and private conversation when she returned to Linton Park. "I want to get this thing settled," he said. "I don't like waiting around. I should like to . . ."

"I will not discuss it, Jack," she had replied. "Not now. Not here. I just want to enjoy the evening with my brother and my cousin. My two cousins," she amended.

Somewhat frustrated, but sure of himself, and willing to wait until she returned home, Ellicott dropped the subject and the party of four had a fine evening although Dunreath tired toward the end of it and they left earlier than they might have under other circumstances. Charlotte, still being jostled by the coach, remembered her private conversation with Dunreath the morning after Aunt Judith's party, just the day before the four of them dined together.

"You look so well, Dunreath. How are you feeling?" They were strolling in the back garden, the children were upstairs doing sums that Charlotte had set for them and she and Dunreath, arm in arm, walked amongst the beautiful flowers Lady Forbes's gardener had grown.

"I have good days and bad. I honestly don't know what to think, Charlotte. I've been to see so many doctors. I went to one yesterday, a specialist of some sort."

"What did he say?"

"He shrugged his shoulders. That's what they all do. Some days, like today, I feel so alive. I just know that I'm going to get well and that Arthur and I will marry and . . . I want so to have a big family like yours—and so does he, I know he does, even though he says it doesn't matter. He's so kind to me, so gentle and I love him so much. Then I have days, whole weeks sometimes, when I can hardly move, when I can't get out of bed, when I just . . ." She started to cry and quickly she wiped the tears from her face. "No, I won't say it, and I won't feel sorry for myself. I have had so much already in life. Arthur and you and all the Lintons and Mama and Papa and Jack. Jack is always good to me. I know some of the things . . . He told me. But don't judge him too harshly."

"I don't judge him at all. It's just that I don't . . ."

"I know. I understand, Charlotte. You don't feel for him the way I do for Arthur. Oh, I wish . . . I wish . . ."

"What?"

"I wish that I could feel the way I do today every day for the rest of my life, even if it turned out to be a short one. But tell me about yourself, Charlotte. I've done nothing but talk about my illness, which has been going on so long now it is a wonder everyone isn't bored to death with it. Tell me about the Forbes and the children and your job. Have you seen much of London? Done much? That was a beautiful gown you were wearing last night. Where did you get it? No, I'm asking too many questions at once. Start at the beginning. The day you arrived. And tell me everything."

Carefully, Charlotte recounted her trip to London and her subsequent meeting with Lady Forbes, her approach to the children, and some of the adventures that had befallen them since her arrival. She just as carefully did not recount her first encounter with Rawley Forbes at the way station, nor of the subsequent meeting by the lake. In fact she did not mention the Marchioness of Kent-Chillingham except in passing as part of her description of the dinner party given by Lady Forbes. Dunreath, however, had known Charlotte since they were both infants and her long years of illness and consequent solitude had made her extremely attuned to moods of others, and especially of her closest friend, Charlotte Linton. Something was not being said and although she was too kind and gentle to allude to that fact directly, she did press Charlotte a little regarding Mr. Rawley Forbes.

"He is a most impertinent young man. I suppose there is worth in him, I don't want to judge him harshly, but there are things that have happened, certain things that I am honor-bound never to repeat, which make me question his sincerity."

"He seemed rather to be watching you a great deal at dinner."

"I can't imagine why. He has made it clear that he detests me."

"Why should he feel that way?"

"It's the incident that I cannot repeat. He blames me for certain things, and then, too, he is a snob. He thinks because I—we—come from the country that we are somehow ill-bred. I think he is a bit of a social climber and persons such as myself are in the way. Then, too, I don't know whether I should repeat this, it is very embarrassing, but it shows the sort of person he is . . ."

"Oh, do tell me, Charlotte. We have always told each other everything, unless of course you have promised not to."

"No, this is something else. We had an argument after the incident that I referred to. At home, late at night . . . I won't go into details but Lisette was sick and I was up and he came home late and we argued. And then . . . I don't know how to say this, quite without warning, he kissed me. I was never so surprised."

Dunreath blushed slightly. "Kissed you, on the mouth?"

"Yes, and it was the . . . oh, I wasn't going to tell you."

"Tell me what?"

"My birthday, the day of my birthday, Jack did the same thing. He wants to marry me, though. Not that his action is forgivable, but at least I suppose one could call it an excuse. But as for Mr. Rawley Forbes, well the less I see of him in the future the better."

But it was not to be.

She must have dozed slightly for the coach continued on and she was not thinking about anything in particular, not about Rawley Forbes or Sophia Kent-Chillingham or the Regent or Beth or Jack or even Dunreath and would she ever completely recover, when she felt someone shaking her arm. It was James and he was saying, "We're here, I believe, where we are to get out. And there is a man down there with a wooden leg who looks like a highwayman."

The ride to Linton Park was over a wide tree-lined road. Already they were on land owned by Henry Linton, her father. She was home. The children were wide-eyed, and perhaps a little terrified of William who had attached his wooden leg for what he evidently considered a special occasion (that was the only time he wore it—on "special occasions"), although in London they had certainly seen enough beggars on the street without limbs. But there was something formidable about William (the leg didn't in any way hamper his movements). He was a large man, rather fierce-looking, and because he spent so much time with the horses a little rough in his manner of speaking.

Charlotte knew that there was not a gentler man in all of Suffolk, but it rather amused her to see these London children so concerned and she decided that she would not tell them anything about William until later on. Certainly, by comparison, the rest of the servants and the Linton family would look docile indeed.

They were just rounding the bend that would lead them to the open space where you could for a moment see the house before the road went back through one more stand of trees when a voice, slightly high-pitched, called out, "Stand and hold. I'll have your money or your lives."

William halted the horses and quickly put his hands in the air. Lisette and James, now thoroughly terrified, threw themselves on the floor of the cart, screaming in fear. Out from behind the bushes stepped two boys, rather tall, with kerchiefs across their faces, both carrying hunting longarms. Charlotte at once recognized her brother G.H. and her cousin, Alfred. She took a deep breath and then started to laugh.

William said, "Thought we'd see if we could throw a fright into you. Come up here you two scamps. I told you she'd know you."

"Char . . ." G.H. called out as he climbed into the cart with Alfie right behind him. They handed their guns to William and then all three embraced. Timorously James and Lisette got up from the floor and were introduced, James red-faced for having shown himself to have been frightened and Lisette still not sure if everything was all right. Both G.H. and Alfie were laughing so hard they couldn't stop.

"And this," Charlotte said, "is how you are greeted by my family. George Henry, you should be ashamed of yourself. And Alfred, you are no better." She put her arms around both boys. "How have you been? How is everyone?"

Alfred answered. "Everyone here is fine. I've been staying with G.H. since Papa and Jack and Dunreath went to London. They came back yesterday, I heard, but I don't want to go home. I'm having too much of a good time here."

"Well, that's up to them and my mother," Charlotte said. "Sit down now, I want to get home."

G.H. said, "No, we'll run ahead and tell them you're coming." He turned to James. "Want to come with us?"

James agreed with alacrity and climbed out of the wagon after G.H. and Alfred. Lisette said she preferred to ride with Charlotte, although she had not, in truth, been asked to join the boys. The three of them ran ahead, out of view, and William started up the horses again.

"I don't know what we're going to do with them two, Miss. And now a third one. Never saw anyone get into so much mischief. The guns wasn't loaded. I saw to that. It was never the same with you girls."

"Oh, I don't know," Charlotte said as much for Lisette's benefit as for William's, "I can remember falling out of trees, all of us did."

"Like James," Lisette said.

"Yes, like James did."

"Well, we've all missed you, Miss Charlotte. Your mother most of all, I think. And the twins. It's not the same without you. Will you be staying now do you think?"

"Only for a few weeks, William. I've a job now, you see."

"But you could be living here, get married to a local, and stay at home. None of my business of course. . . ."

She ignored his servility. She had known him all her life and she supposed that in a way it was his business. "I don't know what I want to do yet and I need to work. Also it was good for me to get away from Suffolk. There are many interesting things in London."

123

William, who had never been any farther than Bury St. Edmonds in one direction and Newmarket in the other, sniffed. "Find all you'll ever need here, I shouldn't wonder."

Charlotte, too, wondered if perhaps he wasn't right. But then she told herself she had not gone to London solely to get away from Suffolk. She had taken a job because it was at least partially necessary. And it was a good thing, too, for her to be on her own. Yes, she might come back to Suffolk to live, back to Linton Park (but not Dunreath Manor, for she was sure she would never marry Jack Ellicott) to spend the rest of her life with her family and friends, the people she knew best, but for now, although she longed to see them and be with them, she knew that she could not stay, that she had to make her own way in the world, and now suddenly she realized, months past her birthday, that she was, indeed a grown-up.

The cart started up the straight path to Linton Park. She could see them there, waiting for her, her mother and sisters and the servants, for G.H. and Alfred and, yes, James, had spread the news. Charlotte Linton was home.

But not, she somehow sensed, ever again to stay.

CHAPTER SIXTEEN

Everyone settled in nicely. She had been home for three days now and the twins had taken to Lisette and she them and G.H. and Alfie had included James in their larks, so much so that Charlotte was afraid he was regressing and she was losing some control of him. It wasn't that the boys were bad, it was just that they didn't seem to be able to find anything to do that wasn't of a mischievous nature. Every scrape in which they were involved led to lectures and minor punishments. It was, after all, the older ones said, just the age. Boys would be boys.

Actually, Charlotte did not have a lot of time for the boys or even for Lisette. It was quite apparent that neither child was going to need to rely on her much, for both were already accepted by the Linton clan. And as this had been a planned vacation she saw no reason to engage them in lessons, and the rudimentary deportment she taught usually referred to a specific incident that had just taken place. And so Charlotte was free to be with Anne, with her mother, and, several days later, when she came for a visit, Dunreath, who was, all in all, looking well. Usually, it was more or less understood that Dunreath did better in the summer months. In the fall, during the mowing season and in the cold winter, her health was poor. In the spring she was better except for a few days in May, when she suffered a kind of relapse. Then, generally throughout June, July, and early August she was well. It was only now July.

Charlotte and Anne were delighted to see her, as was Margaret Linton. Dunreath was everyone's favorite.

"Arthur will be here tomorrow," Dunreath said. "He is bringing a friend with him," she added playfully, eyeing Charlotte.

"Mother didn't tell me that," Charlotte replied. "She just said that he had finished whatever it was he had to do in London and was now on official leave for two weeks and was coming home."

"Everything is happening at once. Father said that the Regent, too, will be in Suffolk tomorrow with a hunting party. Father supposes that we will have to entertain him but not until Mother gets back, which is next week. Cedric will be in the group and so will your friend, Mr. Forbes."

Anne looked up with interest. "Is he related to James and Lisette, Char? You didn't mention you had a friend named Forbes."

"He is their cousin. And I would not call him a friend. He is of marriageable age, so if he comes here I will introduce you, although, I warn you, he is a terrible snob." Anne was always talking about marriage.

"No, I want to meet Arthur's friend. The one he is bringing. I think I like uniforms. What is his name, Dunreath?"

Dunreath took a letter from her sleeve. "A foreign name. Let me see . . . Edward Delacour. French name."

"Of the heart," Anne translated. "That sounds nice. Too bad he is in the Navy. Traveling all the time. Away from home."

"I remember Caroline saying she wanted a man who was away most of the time, so if you don't want him, Anne . . ." Charlotte left the sentence hanging in the air.

"Well, I'll look him over. But if he is really handsome then I suppose you'll change *your* mind."

"No. I'm to marry a London dandy."

Dunreath said, "What are you talking about. You said . . ."

"Anne's prediction. She doesn't even remember. Look at her face. The night of my birthday, Anne, right here in this bedroom, you predicted that I would marry a London dandy within the year."

"Did I? How clever of me. And you've already met one, haven't you? This Mr. Forbes."

"Well, I shall never marry him, that's for certain." Charlotte thought for a moment. "Besides, he would never have me. So it is out of the question."

Anne looked across her sister to Dunreath. "Sounds serious," she said.

Dunreath smiled. "I wonder what we should talk about if we didn't talk of young men."

"After we're married," Anne said, "we'll talk of babies and crops and baking and a new roof, so we'd best talk about young men as long as we can. Except for Charlotte. Married to a rich dandy, I suppose she'll spend all her time in salons talking of music and plays and books and all the latest gossip. Tell me some gossip, Char? From London."

"I don't know any."

"None at all? Why are you blushing?" Anne teasingly pushed her sister, "You *do* know something."

"But it's a secret and not mine to tell, ever. And I only found that out by accident. Besides, I believe it is over."

"A love affair? Truly?"

"No, I don't think so. Just a flirtation. But I refuse to say more. I have given my word."

"Well, I shall never know any true London gossip, then. Will I meet the Prince, do you suppose?"

"He'll be coming to Dunreath Manor, Father says. With a few friends. Not the whole hunting party. I'll see that you are invited, Anne. You and Charlotte and your mother and father, of course, will be there. Father says he supposes it will have to be done. Mother is coming home just to attend to it. It will be a very gala event."

"I can hardly wait," Anne said. "How about you, Char? What are you thinking?"

"Nothing."

"She's wondering if her Mr. Forbes will be there. Was he invited?"

"To the hunt? I believe so."

"Well, perhaps the Regent will bring him along."

Charlotte said, "Oh, I hope not."

Back in London, the Regent's hunting party was leaving. There were twenty-five gentlemen in all. And, although it is true that they were mostly bachelors and mostly younger by a considerable number of years than the Prince, still there were a few older, married men present, including Sir James Forbes. Sir James had no intention of shooting and thus showing himself up, but felt that it was necessary that he accept not only for social, political, and financial reasons, but because Rawley, too, had been included through Sir James's machinations. The Marquis of Kent-Chillingham had also been invited. At first he claimed indisposition, but then he became well enough to accompany the Regent and the sixteen carriages that carried the men and their luggage to Suffolk along the same route that Charlotte had traveled only a week before.

In the Royal carriage was Prince George and his best and only friend and boon companion, the arbiter of all that was fashionable for men to wear (and much of what was fashionable for them to do), Beau Brummell.

The Regent, for a while, slept. The night's adventures had barely ended. Now it was just past ten in the morning and he had been awake most of the time, drinking and gaming. Brummell was wide awake. He seemed never to tire for he had been up exactly the same amount of time as his sovereign. Of course, he was a bit younger (sixteen years to be exact) than the Regent who was soon to turn fifty. Brummell was also, as usual, perfectly attired. Prinny looked like he hadn't changed clothes for three days, whereas, in fact, he had dressed in fresh garments only an hour earlier. The Beau, as he was called, smiled at Prinny, who, mouth-agape, was snoring slightly. The hunting party might be amusing, but if it was a fiasco, he could not be blamed. It had not been his idea, but Prinny's. Brummell had remained noncommittal throughout while the arrangements were being made. If anything went wrong, if it turned out to be a monumental bore (and Brummell was sure it would) he would not be tainted. He saw his task in life as pleasing Prinny. He did his best. But he would never have suggested a royal hunt in, of all places, Suffolk. Unless Prinny was hunting bigger game. One never knew for sure. He was the Regent's confidante, but even he was not told everything.

He sighed and leaned back and closed his eyes, telling himself that as long as the accommodations were good and it didn't rain too much, he was prepared to make the best of the situation. The other gentlemen in the party, at least the younger ones, were all excited, about what he wasn't sure. In truth he seldom got excited about anything. Perhaps that was why he was Prinny's favorite.

As befitted the royal personage, his coach went first so that the dust (which was not inconsiderable) would not bother his person. For that reason alone, Brummell was grateful that he was Prinny's favorite. The job had its compensations. Yes, he always thought of it as a job, currying favor with the Regent. Yet he liked Prinny, too. Sometimes he wondered how long it would last, their friendship. Royalty was known to be fickle. Their friendship had already lasted longer than Brummell suspected was average. That was partly because he stayed as much as possible out of politics. Oh, he had to listen to ministers with their little power plans, he had to pass on messages, occasionally he was even asked for advice (which he always gave reluctantly). Once in a while, he had to do a favor, bring the right person in contact with Prinny, act as a broker as it were. Just what he had done with Sir James Forbes. Prinny got the loan, Forbes got the "Sir," and everyone was happy. Of course that wasn't the end of it. Little favors were always asked for, little extras. The invitation for the cousin, Rawley, for instance. Sir James had approached him and he had smiled and winked and said it would be taken care of. And so it was. Now, Sir James—and Mr. Rawley—Forbes were beholden to Beau Brummell. It was a good plan; you never knew when you might need a friend, or a favor.

He heard Prinny stirring and opened his eyes. There was still a long way to go. Of course there would be several stops before Newmarket where they would bed down for the night. Two inns had been booked. Stops for calls of nature and for food and drink. It was going to be a long, boring trip, but by breaking it up, everyone hoped that it would seem to move quickly. Brummell doubted it. He doubted a lot of things. For instance, he doubted that the Regent was paying for the party. He had heard rumors of a subscription, no doubt an oversubscription with the residue going into the royal pocket. And a good time would be had by all. Well, what was money for, except to buy pleasure? He had never had enough of it. Money or pleasure. But he wasn't doing badly. He could hardly complain. And so far, he had resisted lining his own pockets. It would not have been hard. A hint to Sir James, for instance, and Rawley Forbes's ticket of admission would have been paid for, the money going into his own coffers. But it wasn't his way; he was not interested in small bribes. There would come a time . . . and in the meanwhile, he was living very comfortably. Of course he owed his tailor a shocking amount, but no gentleman ever paid his tailor. Well, he might pay him, but always very late and only when new clothes were needed and had to be ordered.

With such thoughts rumbling around in his head, he, too, finally joined the Regent in a fitful but not unpleasant sleep.

They did stop twice and both stops, which should have taken under an hour, each consumed more than two hours so that when they finally arrived in Newmarket it was nearly midnight and the Prince (not to mention the rest of the party) was edgy. No one seemed to want to go bed and so the public rooms of both inns contained a rare sight: elegantly dressed gentlemen from London drinking from tankards and carrying on conversations from wooden tables while eating country fare mostly with their hands. It was a boisterous night, for the two inns were only a few yards apart and there was much traveling back and forth between the two. Several card games were started and seemed still to be going on as dawn crept up on the Suffolk countryside, while the rest of the gentlemen slept.

One of the cardplayers was Rawley Forbes. It was not in his nature to leave any group first, nor ever to turn down any invitation that might in some way test what he considered his manhood. His cousin, older and wiser, had long before retired.

Rawley was on a winning streak; the cards were falling for him. Also, he had wisely had less to drink than any of his opponents and they were making foolish bets, taking unnecessary chances, while he, for a change, was being quite practical, conscious that, although he was certainly not cheating, he did in a way have an unfair advantage over the other young men.

Finally, as the sun began to streak the card table, several of the gentlemen vowed that they were tired and that quite obviously they were not going to recoup any of their losses. "Not this day, Forbes, I should say, but you'll give us another chance soon?"

"Any time, gentlemen. Tonight, if you wish. I'm more than willing to continue. . . ."

The one who had been speaking to him yawned. "No. Enough. Enough cards. Enough drink. Just need sleep. We all do. Come along you losers, we're off to bed. Forbes can pay the tab. Right, old man?"

"Only too happy. I'll be up presently."

And he fully intended to do just that, pay the innkeeper who was asleep in the corner and then retire himself. But he hated to wake the old man so instead he decided, as the sun was just up, he would take a brisk walk to clear his head, then come back, wake the man, pay the bill, and go off to sleep. The hunt was not starting until the next day.

It was a crackling nice morning. The air was cool and crisp, dew was on the grass. The sun was just over the tops of the houses down the road that led to Bury St. Edmonds. Come to think of it, wasn't the Linton house—Linton Park, was that what it was called?—in that direction? Some distance off. God, he thought, how dreary, to live the rural life. He could hear animals. The horses in the stables, cows somewhere not far off, and the inevitable rooster had been crowing since before the game broke up. There was another sound, too. A coach and four, he believed. The night coach from where? His ears were not finely enough tuned to tell yet from which direction the sound was coming.

The coach was coming from London, for he finally saw the dust on the London road. He was near the side of the inn when the coach came to a stop. Three gentlemen climbed wearily down. One of them he recognized at once, for he had met him only several weeks before and in his naval uniform he stood out. It was Arthur Linton, brother of the girl he detested so. There was another young man with him, also in his ensign's blue, and the two of them stretched their legs and looked around while the third passenger, obviously an important personage, stayed close to the carriage.

The two naval men went inside while the youth who tended the horses came forward and spoke with the driver and then unhitched the beasts. The important personage continued to stare at the inn. He had not seen Rawley, in fact, none of them had. Rawley examined him more closely. His, too, was a familiar face. It was the Earl of Liverpool, the leader of the opposition in the Parliament. Had he come to join the hunt? Moments later, Beau Brummell came out the front door, said something to the two officers who immediately went inside.

Brummell went to the coach and spoke to the man standing there. Then without warning or fanfare the Prince Regent stepped out into the chilly morning air and walked quickly to the coach. He was helped inside by Brummell

131

and the Earl of Liverpool followed him while Brummell, acting as a sort of guard, stayed outside. Obviously some business of state, Rawley told himself, wishing that he could find out what it was. He was on the far side of the coach and could not be seen, he was sure, so he moved as close as he could. Brummell stood with his back to him, watching the inn. Rawley was able to slip up to the back of the coach. The side window was open and he could hear their voices.

"Yes," the Regent was saying, "I will support you."

The other voice, one Rawley Forbes had never heard, high-pitched and whining, answered, "And I will do what Spencer will not do. I will see that your allowance limitation is removed. What Pitt suggested long ago. We cannot tell about your father—God bless the King—but I feel that you should be free, sir . . ."

"And you want to be Prime Minister."

"I should think anyone would be preferable to Spencer Perceval."

"From my point of view, yes. But you are an admirable choice, Liverpool."

"It is done then. It will take some time. We cannot call a question in the House—one that will bring the government down until, well, it will be the better part of a year."

"I can wait. I've waited this long. You had best leave now, before you are seen."

"Yes. It will be a long trip back."

"But a worthwhile one."

Rawley Forbes ducked back to his position at the side of the inn just before the Regent got out, nodded to Brummell, and went inside.

He knew he possessed a valuable piece of information, one that he could not disclose to just anyone, but for the moment he did not see how he could use it. But then he told himself, perhaps someday I will need a favor. From someone. Whistling he started down the road toward Bury St. Edmonds. He wanted to take a long walk and be sure that no one was up when he got back.

CHAPTER SEVENTEEN

A week later, while preparations were underway at Dunreath Manor for a dinner party to be given by the Ellicotts (as the wealthiest and most genteel of Suffolk gentry) for the Regent and a few of his friends, the hunt was going on. In fact it was going on quite close to Linton Park, and Rawley Forbes, somewhat to the south of the main group, found himself looking up at a house about a quarter of a mile away and seeing strolling from it toward him three familiar figures and one, a woman, whose face he didn't recognize but whom he would have wagered all that he had won the past week was related to Charlotte Linton. It was, indeed Charlotte, her brother Arthur, and the other naval officer whom he recognized. The other lady was, he would soon find out, Charlotte's younger sister, Anne.

Rawley, a careful hunter, checked the breech of his gun to make sure that it was not primed and loaded and then stood waiting for them. He would hear calls in the distance as some of the other members of the party were moving off in a more northerly direction, but he had no inclination to follow them. In fact, the whole week had been a bore. Had it not been for his phenomenal run of luck at cards in the evening (a run that was beginning to make some of the losers grumble and look at him with side-long glances), he would have wished he had not come. The closest he had been to the Regent the whole time was when he overheard the conversation in the carriage. Prinny had not spoken to him once, had not even acknowledged his presence. It was almost as if he knew that Rawley had done something unforgivable, eavesdropping that way, and was waiting for a time to chastise him in front of everyone, perhaps banish him from the hunt and from London.

Also, Rawley had bagged nothing of importance and hunting without at least an occasional flush and kill was doubly a nuisance. The accommodations were satisfactory but a bit primitive, and the food, although good and wholesome, was eaten in such a noisy atmosphere that often as not he had a headache before he sat down to play cards. And he had to play every night to give the losers their chance to win. He liked being far ahead, wanted to keep as much of the winnings as possible, but it wouldn't do to be thought a greedy player or a card cheat. Tonight, he told himself, he would deliberately lose some of it back. Then tomorrow night perhaps he could sleep.

There was one other thing. He had not been invited to attend the small party being given by the Ellicotts for the Prince. It was not, he knew, their fault. Prinny had made up, with Brummell's help, the list. Rawley Forbes had not even been considered. How, he wondered, could he get in the Beau's good graces?

The party of four from the house on the hill, obviously Linton Park, called out to him. He waved back in return and stood waiting until they assayed the curving path and came to where he was standing.

He shook hands with Arthur, bowed to Charlotte, and was introduced to Charlotte's sister, Anne, and Ensign Edward Delacour. He respectively bowed and shook hands.

They asked him how the hunt was going and he replied that his bag was empty. And that he was rather behind the others and in no mood to catch up. Arthur Linton suggested he join them on their walk which, he explained, would be rather circular, taking them back to Linton Park where he could partake of some nourishment and then they would see that he got back to wherever he was going. Arthur was already too much the diplomat to ask if Mr. Forbes would be going to Dunreath Manor or back to Newmarket where the group was lodged.

Although he surprised himself by doing it, Rawley accepted with alacrity and a certain amount of pleasure. He longed for civilized company. It was only somewhat later as they neared the house that it occurred to him that at least some of the Lintons would be going to Dunreath Manor and that he would be an embarrassment to them and would be embarrassed himself. But it was too late. He had already accepted their offer for luncheon.

Arthur performed the introductions; the Linton family, all of whom who were present were just sitting down to lunch. But before he could get started James and Lisette ran to their cousin, engulfed him with hugs and insisted that he listen to each of them tell what a marvelous time they were having on their vacation in the country. Finally, the children were settled down, an extra place laid for the guest, and everyone sat down to eat. Before the food was passed, though, Henry Linton said a simple grace, they all echoed "Amen," and then the conversation and the passing of the viands began simultaneously.

"And how is the Regent faring?" Mr. Linton asked their guest as he handed him a plate with a huge slice of cold beef. "Does he enjoy himself? I should have thought by now he would have tired of the hunt."

"I am not privy to his thoughts or even to his counsel. He seems to be faring well, though. He is a crack shot and most of the young bucks are hard-pressed to match him. I, myself, have done very poorly at shooting. Not enough practice, I should say. But he does not seem restless or bored." Rawley did not add that the Regent had been up earlier than anyone, meeting the coach from London, and presumably various important people. He, Rawley, had been unable to get a close view again, the way he had the first day. "He seems to like it here, a change perhaps from the city. Each day he is enthusiastic, at least as he starts off. As I said, I am not an intimate. I suppose I was rather lucky to have been invited at all."

"Then you won't be coming to Dunreath Manor tonight?" Henry Linton asked the question in such a natural manner that Rawley was not, as he thought he might have been, the least bit put off.

"I'm afraid not, Sir. Although I should like it, if only to renew the acquaintance of the Ellicotts who so graciously invited my whole family to dine, where I met your son, Arthur."

"Yes, of course. Well, he won't be going, either. Just Margaret and myself and Charlotte. Not even Anne, who is quite put out, aren't you, Anne? One young lady from each household in the district, my sister-in-law told me. Strict orders via this Brummell fellow. Dunreath will be there and Charlotte and my wife and I. And the Ellicotts, that will include Jack but not Alfred. Poor Judith and George. I

135

fear they are going to have their hands full. Glad he didn't choose us, eh, Margaret?"

"Yes, indeed. I've already baked a considerable amount to take with me and so have several others. We're leaving directly after lunch. Of course we will have to change clothes first. We won't be back until quite late. Perhaps we shall have to stay over. Oh, I hope the Prince and his party aren't, not that there isn't the room but still. . . . Poor Judith. You are most welcome to stay here, Mr. Forbes. Rather than going all the way back to Newmarket."

"Oh, I wouldn't want to impose."

"No imposition at all," Henry Linton said. "Got the room. Got your young cousins there. Stay the night. Someone will be driving to Newmarket tomorrow. You can ride along."

Lisette and James chorused, "Do stay, Rawley. It will be so much fun." And then everyone joined in. He had to admit that he wanted to accept the invitation. He would get a good night's sleep, he would not have to play cards, and he would not have to show up at Newmarket and be in the company of the others left behind, the second-class guests of the Regent, as he had already begun to think of them.

And Arthur, too, pressed him to stay. Only Charlotte Linton was silent, but then she was not even going to be present, which made it an even more attractive offer. Gratefully and graciously he accepted. James gave a whoop of joy and the whole family laughed.

Standing on the steps, Rawley Forbes joined the family in seeing off their parents and Charlotte. He envied them already, their easy comraderie, the way they so obviously cared for one another, the closeness of their relationships. And he could see that James and Lisette had been accepted into the family group and had seemingly adjusted themselves already. The Lintons were a close-knit family and an open one that was quite willing to accept anyone who happened along the way. His estimation of them was high and his estimation of Miss Charlotte Linton had already gone up some. In retrospect, he could see that he really had little or no right to be angry with her. Quite obviously she had not been spying on him and Sophia. Sophia. He had hardly thought of her for a week. Instead, he admitted to himself, he had quite often thought of Miss Linton. And he was now not sure that it was accident alone that drew him so close to her house that morning. And now she was leaving, going to Dunreath Manor, a few miles away, to mix with Prinny and Beau and all of the men (mostly older ones, including his cousin Sir James, he had to admit) who had been invited. At that moment he would gladly have exchanged all of his luck at cards the past week for that one invitation. She would be there among some of his friends and, what was worse, Jack Ellicott, whom he had instinctively seen as a suitor to Miss Linton's hand, would be there, too. It was no wonder that he looked a little depressed when Arthur Linton spoke to him and suggested that he join Arthur and Edward for a walk to the stables. One of the mares was sickly. And Arthur wanted Rawley's advice about several of the stallions.

Rawley understood this as merely a kindness to a stranger, but he quickly accepted and so the three young men went off to the stables, the domain of William Clapp, who was hobbling about again, having put his wooden leg aside.

They spent some time in the stable. Clapp obviously enjoyed their company and enjoyed showing off his horses and his own knowledge. Rawley found that he liked Arthur Linton very much. The young man was only a year or so his senior, and his companion, Delacour, a little older, was himself well-known in London society. He was a rather quiet young man and seemed to be observing Rawley.

Perhaps, Rawley thought, he has come as a suitor, too, to Miss Linton. Well, it is none of my business. Let them fight over her, she is nothing to me—worse luck.

After spending an hour in the stable, the three men bid Will Clapp a good day and began to amble back toward the house. They could hear noise from the yard, the children, no doubt, playing games. But no one was in sight. Delacour stopped for a moment as though to examine something on the ground and they waited for him.

"We wanted to talk to you—alone," Delacour said. "It was fortuitous that you came by this day. We were almost certain we would see you. In fact we had planned to come this very afternoon to Newmarket, since so many people will be at Dunreath Manor."

"Yes," Forbes said. "Well, I am at your disposal."

"You saw what happened the morning we arrived," Arthur said.

"I don't know what . . ."

"Please," Delacour interrupted. "Let me explain our position. My father is rather important in the Admiralty. I have served a while longer than Arthur, but both of us have been entrusted by my father with a mission. We came north on the same coach as . . . well, as His Lordship. No names need be mentioned. Our job was simply to see that he was not bothered and not recognized. He had an important meeting. After the meeting, we saw, or rather Arthur saw, you walking down the road. He was watching from a second-story window. From that we have to presume that you were up early and about. And that no doubt you saw and perhaps heard what took place. There is a spy on the hunting trip. That is, someone sent there by the P.M. to take note of everything the Regent does. It is natural that we suspect you."

"Gentlemen, I assure you . . . Yes, I was up that morning. Hadn't been to bed, dammit. Playing cards, had a good run of luck, went out for some air and your coach came along. I was not in view and I saw no reason to announce myself. But I was not spying for the P.M. Yes, I did recognize the . . . the other gentleman. But I have mentioned the fact to no one." Which was true enough. But he *had* thought of using the information. Now, they thought he might be a spy.

"Word has it that you are up and about early *each* morning."

"It seems the P.M. is not the only one with a spy in the ranks. I told you I have been playing cards. I've had a streak of winning. . . . Well, you know how it is, a gentleman simply can't quit. So I have played every night and had slept little. Yes, I have been up at dawn, I confess that."

"And today, when the Prince won't be at Newmarket and therefore cannot meet anyone, you have decided to stay away. You tried hard to get an invitation to Dunreath Manor, I'm told." It was Mr. Delacour who was doing all the talking. Arthur Linton merely watched them, as if he was afraid that Rawley Forbes might bolt and run.

"Of course I wanted to be invited. But I hadn't a chance.

The Prince doesn't know I'm alive. My cousin, Sir James, was invited and so were most of the older gentlemen. . . ."

"Including Kent-Chillingham?"

"Yes, I believe so, why?"

"You've been seeing his wife."

"Now look here . . ."

"Haven't you?"

"In the past. It was a flirtation, that's all. I have not seen her, well, since several weeks before I left London. I think we are not on speaking terms." He paused for a moment and then asked, "What has that to do with . . . ? Do you mean the Marquis . . . ?"

"It is important to some people that the King, no matter how ill, not pass on his powers. That is foolhardy. The Regent may not possess all the admirable qualities that a monarch *should* possess, but he is all we have. There is trouble across the sea, in America. . . . And France is preparing to go to war in Europe. We need a strong man at the helm. At least one who is not a . . . dithering imbecile."

"But I don't understand."

"Listen to me, Mr. Rawley Forbes. Certain men could make an extreme amount of money if the powers are not passed on. And England could lose much. This cousin of yours, has he not entered into a business arrangement with the Marquis of Kent-Chillingham?"

"I believe so. I don't know much about it. But James is not a traitor, I assure you. He is the most loyal subject."

"Yes, I believe he is." Arthur Linton spoke for the first time. "And I believe Mr. Forbes is a loyal subject, too. We know who our man is, Edward."

"Yes, but I want to be sure. Mr. Forbes, you can help us. Kent-Chillingham is the man. The spy. He is reporting directly to Perceval. We can hardly stop him. So far he has done nothing treasonous. But he must be watched."

"And my cousin?"

"No, we'll take your word on that. I doubt he knows what he has gotten himself into. The Marquis does not have the money he pretends to have, which is one reason why he is doing what he is doing. Your cousin, Sir James, had best beware. We shan't bother him. But we need your help. Something important may happen at Dunreath Manor."

"You don't mean that he would . . ."

"Oh, good Lord man, no. No one is going to assassinate Prinny. But if it were known that he has been seeing the Earl . . . a certain gentleman, a question might come up in Parliament and Spencer Perceval would almost certainly prevail."

"But what can I do?"

"Ride to Dunreath Manor."

"But I haven't been invited."

"Play the fool. . . . Do anything to get in. Say you have come because . . . I say, I have it. Say you have come because of Arthur's sister, Miss Linton. You know her quite well. Play the gallant. Act the fool. Do what you will. But get to Brummell and tell him that the Prince must not sleep tonight at Dunreath Manor as was planned."

"But the Prince . . ."

"I assure you, after the Prince finds out what you have done for him, you will not have to worry."

"But what is supposed to happen?"

"Another meeting. Only this time it will be observed and reported. The meeting can only be stopped if the Prince is not present. If you can get him to leave, which I doubt, so much the better. But Brummell will be able to do it. So get to Brummell. Pretend to woo Miss Linton, they will all forgive you for that, but get to Brummell."

CHAPTER EIGHTEEN

As he rode toward Dunreath Manor, Rawley Forbes felt more and more like a fool. They had told him to act the fool, but it wouldn't be necessary to act (not that he could have, had he wanted to; he detested the idea of actors), for what he was doing was so foolish and so embarrassing that he did not know how he could carry it off. On top of it all, Miss Charlotte Linton! How could he pretend to wish to woo her when . . . He didn't know what to think. He hated her one moment and had entirely different feelings the next.

But to do something like this! Why had he ever let them talk him into doing this? Because he was afraid, he answered. They had hinted they thought him a spy and that could ruin everything for his future. Besides, in a way he had been spying and he felt guilt about that, too. And so he had acquiesced. Now he was riding like a highwayman across Suffolk toward Dunreath Manor, to try to get a message to the Prince. No, just to Brummell. But he couldn't, they had told him, simply burst in and demand to see the Prince. That would scare away the real spy and for some reason there was a plan afoot where the Prince would not be compromised but his adversary or adversaries would be discovered and put in such an untenable position that they would not be able to do him harm again.

Forbes was perspiring. It was a hot day and he was moving rather quickly on the horse, but he knew that wasn't the real reason. He was frightened. His whole future might depend on just what happened next.

He told himself to try to concentrate, to decide exactly how he was going to approach the problem. The problem, as he saw it, was Miss Charlotte Linton.

That good young woman, meanwhile, after arriving at Dunreath Manor and going with her mother to the kitchen to see if there was any help she could offer was now standing with Dunreath and several other young ladies of the area, engaged in conversation with the man she had met at the Forbes's, the Marquis of Kent-Chillingham, Mr. Beau Brummell, and Sir James Forbes. Only a few feet away, Jack Ellicott, pretending to talk to several other young ladies and one gentleman from London, was scowling at her across the room.

Twice he had tried to get her attention, but she simply smiled at him by way of a greeting and went on with her conversation. The Prince was in the huge hall, too, but at the far end, in polite conversation with George and Judith Ellicott and Cedric Fitzhugh. The rest of the party was scattered about the room and some of them had spilled out onto the lawn, for it was a glorious day. The Regent and his entourage had arrived only an hour before and, after refreshing themselves, had joined the group in the main hall of Dunreath Manor. It was a peculiar party in that the city gentlemen so obviously were more fashionably dressed than the country women, yet the young women, from the best families in Suffolk, several of them even titled, were far more at ease than the men. If country and city were meeting, perhaps because they were on their home ground, the country ladies had the distinct advantage. Oddly enough, they were not awed by the presence of the Regent. Deferentially polite, of course, but not at all frightened by the fact that most of them were seeing him for the first time, they seemed (as was the case with Charlotte Linton) to the manor born. And they were determined that, no matter what, they would not be thought country bumpkins by these city gentlemen. And so the conversation was gay, the laughter frequent, and not at all the boring event that Beau Brummell had predicted to himself.

It was he who suggested that their little group move outside. By that time the Ellicotts and the Regent had been joined by Henry and Margaret Linton. The Regent, at Henry Linton's suggestion, agreed that it was a bit close inside, so they, too, went out onto the terrace that overlooked the main road between Newmarket and Bury St. Edmonds. Within a few minutes the thirty or so people who made up the party were now all on the lawn. Had

Rawley Forbes been following the main road, his approach would have been observed by all of them for the last mile of his journey. But he was taking a back way, suggested by Arthur Linton, just to meet such a contingency. Rawley and his somewhat weary horse were now picking their way along a narrow by-way that followed a stream that would, if he found the right fork in the path, lead him to the out buildings behind Dunreath Manor, where hopefully he could leave the horse and, unseen, approach the house from the rear.

Of course once he got there he could hardly hide. For one thing he was still in his hunting clothes. Arthur Linton had offered him a change of wardrobe but they were not of a size, especially across the chest, and they could find nothing for Rawley to wear that even approximated a good fit.

He had worked out a plan, not a very satisfactory one, to be sure, but it was the best that he could think of at the moment. It would perhaps get him to Brummell and would (again perhaps) keep him from seeming a total idiot. But it all depended on luck and Miss Charlotte Linton. His luck had been good lately, but his relationship with Miss Linton had been exactly the opposite. He would have to tell her something, although he had been cautioned by Delacour to let no one know what he was about. Still, if she would only listen . . .

The path had narrowed so he dismounted. He easily found the way that cut up from the stream. In the distance he could hear noise. He was, he judged, no more than a half-mile from his destination and his fate.

They had been spaced in small groups inside; somehow on the lawn, although a few groups moved away, a central core seemed to form with, not unnaturally, the Prince Regent at its center. About half of the party was in this one group, including Charlotte Linton and Jack Ellicott. Prinny was telling the story of a visit he had made as a child many years ago to the same area in the company of his father. He had hated it, he said, because he had been stung by a bee and then to add insult to royal injury, while playing in a field he had stepped into . . . well, politeness kept him from using the word, but everyone present knew what he meant. "From that time forward, I hated the countryside.

But today, I must say I am glad to be back. Provided I don't get stung or make a misstep."

Henry Linton asked him how well the hunting had been going and that got the Regent started on another topic, for he, it seemed, had bagged so much game that the young men were complaining that it was being cooked each night and fed to them for supper. "Someone suggested I should shoot a cow," the Prince said and everyone laughed. It was obvious that Prinny was enjoying himself and that he was making friends in Suffolk. He was far less starchy than the country folk had been led to believe. Even the notorious Brummell was turning out to be a gentleman with very few pretensions, despite his overly modish attire.

In short, the party was going well, and Judith Ellicott, and to a lesser extent her husband who simply expected everything to go well, was relieved. There was more than enough food, enough to have fed his whole party, Judith told herself, and it was not all game, fortunately, for from what the Prince had said the gentlemen had had enough game to last them for a while.

Of course it would be a long time until they ate and many things could go wrong, but on such a beautiful day and with everyone in such spirits, she was sure that nothing untoward could possibly take place. Naturally she was not aware that at the very moment she was thinking those thoughts, Rawley Forbes was tethering his horse in the stables only a few hundred yards from the kitchen entrance to Dunreath Manor. The stable boy, who surely was a halfwit for he had not spoken since Rawley's arrival, watched with his mouth open even wider than his eyes.

Rawley put his finger to his lips to caution the young man to say nothing and then when the horse was safely stalled and happily chomping on some straw, Rawley put his arm around the young man's shoulder and led him aside into a dark recess of the interior of the huge stables.

"Do you know Miss Charlotte Linton?" he asked.

The boy answered in something that sounded like a foreign language. When finally Rawley had sorted out the words, he assumed the answer to be, "Of course I do. Been here all my life." What he actually heard, though, was, "Orsetoben Earal Maliff." The boy seemed to pause between every other word. It wasn't a stutter. Just a thinking out how to formulate the next words.

"Can you get word to her? See her alone? Take her a message?"

"Missuge. Sher."

"A message. Sure. Good for you. Tell her . . . No, I'd best write it down. Have you pen and paper?"

The boy grinned as if to say, what would he be needing paper and pen in the stable for? Still, he took Rawley by the hand and led him to a small boarded-off area that must have served as an office. There was, among the broken tack and rusted pieces of iron, a small table and on it was an inkwell, a quill, and some scraps of paper, old bills no doubt. It was here that the head stableman figured out his accounts. Today, no doubt, he was busy up at the house. In a way, Rawley was glad. The boy was stupid, but he would not cause trouble or ask embarrassing questions. And it was likely that he could not read, so the missive sent to Miss Linton, unless interrupted on its journey, would not be seen by other eyes.

He sat down and quickly started to write:

My Dear Miss Linton:
Please forgive me for imposing on you in this manner. I can explain nothing on paper, but it is urgent that I speak with you alone as soon as possible. I shall have to wait below here in the stable from whence I am writing this, for my appearance at the house would cause confusion and many more questions than I can safely answer. Please be assured that it is an important matter or I would not ask for your help, nor interfere with the good time I am sure you are having. Please come for the message I bear is not from myself alone but from your brother, Arthur, as well.
            Yr. ob. serv.

Then he signed his name with a flourish, folded the scrap of paper, which was not that attractive but was the best he could find, handed it to the boy with a half crown, and told him to get the letter to Miss Linton but try not to be seen doing it. And to go as fast as he could.

The boy bit the coin, pocketed it, took the letter, and waved to Rawley from the doorway. Then he trudged slowly up the path. Rawley wanted to scream out, "Hurry, you little monster," but he held his tongue. He was on unfamiliar terrain. Perhaps the boy knew what he was doing. Hurrying might draw attention to the lad. Well, he told himself, there was nothing to do now but wait. But he couldn't relax and so he moved out in the area between the stalls and stared at the horses who, balefully, stared back at him.

By dint of only a slight maneuver, Jack Ellicott had managed to draw Charlotte aside and away from the group that surrounded the Prince.

"Are you enjoying yourself?" he asked.

"Yes, I suppose so. It is a beautiful day and everyone seems very pleasant. Aunt Judith has organized everything beautifully. How did you enjoy London?"

"Outside of the fact that I hardly saw you, very much. I could easily get accustomed to the London life."

"And I don't think I ever could. Yes, I suppose I could, as long as I could come home for a visit every few months. I would be like Aunt Judith . . . some time here, some time there."

"It might be possible," he said.

"It *is* possible right now. I think Lady Forbes would be pleased to have me bring the children to Linton Park for a visit every few months, weeks, even."

"Yes, but you won't be with her . . . them . . . forever."

"No, that's true. But there might be others."

"Look here, Charlotte, you're not really planning to make a career out of this governess thing. I mean, it isn't necessary. You've been away, seen London, had a good time. But you should think of the future."

"Please, Jack, don't spoil the day."

"My days have been spoiled for a long time."

"I'm sorry but I really think you should put me out of your mind."

"I could never do that."

The stable boy came walking across the lawn and seemed to be heading straight for them. He got to within a few feet and then stopped. Annoyed, Jack said, "Well, what do you want? Can't you see I'm busy. If it's about the horses, I really can't be bothered. . . ."

"I've a message," the lad answered.

"Oh, well, what is it?"

"For Miss Linton."

"For Miss Linton. Here she is. Go ahead, you oaf, say what you have to say."

"I ain't to say it. It's writ down. And it's private," he added.

He held out the note but before Charlotte could take it, Ellicott had snatched it from the boy's hand.

"Jack!" Charlotte protested.

But he had already unfolded it and was busily reading the contents, which were quite short, before she could even attempt to wrest it from him.

His face red with anger, he handed it to her. "Oh, yes, of course! All you want to be is a governess. All the time in London with that dandy! Well, we'll see about him."

Charlotte was busy reading the note as Ellicott started toward the stable area. "Jack," she called out. "Please."

He stopped for a moment and turned. He had heard his name called twice and when he looked back he saw his father and the Regent coming toward Charlotte. Reluctantly, he walked back.

George Ellicott performed the introductions. "Sir, this is my son, Jack Ellicott. And this is Miss Charlotte Linton, Henry Linton's daughter, of Linton Park."

Jack bowed as Charlotte curtsied.

"Dear me," the Prince said, "we seem to have interrupted something. I do apologize, but I was admiring you from afar, Miss Linton. I understand you are Lady Fitzhugh's niece, which makes you Ceddy's cousin. He told me you were staying in London with Sir James Forbes. A nice family, I think."

"Yes, indeed, Sir."

"Don't let us prevent you from leaving, Mr. Ellicott. I believe you were heading . . ."

"I was going to the stable. The boy brought a message. But it is probably not important."

"Probably not. Miss Linton, I wonder if you would do me the honor to show me about the grounds. You are here, the Ellicotts tell me, almost as much as you are at your own home. And more than you are in London. I should hope that we might see more of you in London."

"I'm not really in society, Sir."

"Well, you should be. I think we could stroll together without it causing too much gossip. Here, you've dropped your letter."

"Just a message, from a friend . . ."

"From far away?"

"No, from Linton Park."

"Excuse us," the Prince said to Ellicott *pere* and *fils*. "We shan't stroll far. I must not show favoritism. One of the hard parts of being royalty, my dear. If I talk to one person for a minute longer than another then a plot is assumed to be afoot. Come along."

When they were out of earshot and had walked a few yards back toward the house but not out of line with the path to the stable he said to her, "There, now I have extricated you from the situation. Don't worry, the Beau is ready to take you for a further stroll. You see, we are expecting a message from your brother's friend, Mr. Delacour. I thought that the *billet doux* you received might just be . . ."

"I'm afraid not, Sir. It is from Mr. Rawley Forbes of your party. He only says that it is urgent that he see me. He has a message from my brother."

"Where are you to meet him?"

"At the stable."

"Fine, we'll walk in that direction and then you can slip away."

"But Jack . . ."

The Regent smiled. "That young man and his father will be well occupied for the next few minutes. I'll see to that. Now you run along down there and I shall return to Mr. Jack Ellicott. I assure you, he will not be coming to the stable. By the way, have you seen the Marquis of Kent-Chillingham?"

"Earlier I saw him with Jack, as a matter of fact."

"Indeed. Well, you go to your rendezvous and find out about this important message. Beau will be nearby. In case you need help. I had some doubts about young Mr. Forbes, but perhaps I was mistaken. Do you like him?"

Her answer surprised her, for she was certain the words did not come from her own mouth yet she heard them clearly, "Yes, yes, I do."

CHAPTER NINETEEN

Miraculously, for he had now assumed that the message had gone undelivered or that the lady had torn it up and thrown it in the boy's face or somesuch, Rawley Forbes saw Miss Charlotte Linton walking down the path toward the stable and she was accompanied by Mr. Beau Brummell! He wanted to wave to them but he decided to wait in the shadows of the stable instead. Before they were halfway down the path, Mr. Brummell stopped, said something to her and sent her on ahead. Rawley would have marveled at his own good fortune (although a part of him was now congratulating himself for his brilliant plan, where only minutes before he was sure that it had been a stupid one and he had failed), had it not been that instead he was marveling at the beauty of Miss Linton, her blonde hair shimmering halo-like in the sun, her chin tilted up, her cheeks pink with the summer air, matching, it suddenly occurred to him, the roses on the bushes so assiduously tended by an unnamed man on Prospect Lane, her form so perfectly proportioned. . . . Well, she was in her natural habitat and perhaps that was why he was smitten so, or perhaps it was just that he had never seen her from afar coming toward him, or perhaps he was just grateful that somehow the serious mission that he had been given and at which he could easily have failed, had turned into an adventure. He was still perspiring, but it was no longer from the heat of the day, his physical exertion or fear. He dared not name the cause, yet she was now only a few yards from his presence.

Lest she be startled, he called out to her, "I am right here, Miss Linton, standing in the shadow. Do not be frightened."

She stopped and stared until her eyes became accustomed to the dark area toward which she was peering and answered, "I am not frightened, Mr. Forbes. Need I be?"

"No, of course. I didn't mean . . ." He found himself unable to articulate a simple sentence. Remembering that he was not supposed to be present at all, he said, "Will you come inside. It . . . it would be better. . . . I see Mr. Brummell above, so . . ."

"I said I was not frightened. Do you not be so, either."

Coolly, almost deliciously, he thought, she stepped from the sunlight into the shadow. She was only a few feet from him and his heart was pounding harder than it had during his entire ride from Linton Park to Dunreath Manor.

"You said you had a message from my brother."

He didn't want the interview to end. He could, he knew, in a few words explain everything or he could simply say that he had come to her to get to Mr. Brummell and as Mr. Brummell was waiting above, would she please send for him. But he could not say those things, not at the moment, for he had suddenly become tongue-tied. He didn't want her to leave ever, and once he spoke, once he explained, she would be gone and . . .

"Well?" He came back to earth, was no longer floating, but still felt a dryness in his throat that made his voice crack, made him croak as he started to speak.

"You read my letter?"

"Of course. That is why I am here. You said it was important. You intimated that my brother had sent you."

"Yes, in a way, he did. He and Mr. . . . Look here, Miss Linton, you don't hate me, do you? I know I must seem—have seemed an awful fool. . . . I presumed so much and I . . . Well I should like to explain at length, but perhaps this isn't the time. . . . Yes, it is. . . . If I can deliver the message."

"I don't hate you. But I do want you to deliver the message, please. And I cannot be away from the others for long."

Why did she sound so cold, so distant? It was his own fault. He had behaved like a cad, a fool, he had been . . . well, he would make amends at once. But first, he must give her the message.

"In point of fact," he said, regaining some of his composure and most of his voice, "Mr. Delacour, your brother's friend, has sent me with an urgent message for the Prince."

"Then why don't you . . . ?"

"That I am to deliver to Mr. Brummell, who is just above. Would you mind asking him to join us. It is a private—secret—message and my job was to get to him without being noticed, an almost impossible task. But then I thought of you . . . that perhaps . . . I know it all seems strange, but if you would signal to him and then after I speak with him . . . Could you? . . . Never mind, I'll explain it to him. I beg of you to trust me and do as I ask. Then wait and I will explain as much as I dare, as he will permit me."

She must have sensed the urgency in his voice, for she did not argue or question him, but instead, walked back out into the sunlight and, as though it had been prearranged, held up her right arm, dropped it to her side, and then repeated the gesture. Immediately, Beau Brummell, who had been casually munching an apple picked from an old tree that stood by the path, a green one that was rather bitter to his mouth but nonetheless tasty, flipped aside the core and sauntered, looking over his shoulder only once when he first started out, toward the stable and, should anyone be watching, seemingly a rendezvous with a certain country lady. He hoped her reputation would not be ruined, should he be seen meeting her this way, but it was by the far the safest plan. If noticed, it would be accepted. The notorious London rake and libertine, Beau Brummell, has an assignation with a simple, innocent country lass.

As soon as he got to the stable door she stepped inside and said, "Mr. Forbes wants, it seems, not me, but you. I shall return to the gathering above."

"Yes, my dear, do, just return to the party as though nothing has happened. Don't worry about your friend. He will cause you no difficulties."

Rawley Forbes's heart sank. "But I wanted to explain to Miss Linton . . . that is, explain what I might. . . . I wanted to talk with her," he trailed off lamely.

"I am afraid what goes on between us must never be repeated, Mr. Forbes. Excuse us, Miss Linton."

"Sir." She curtsied. "Mr. Forbes. Your servant."

"Mayn't I . . . ?" But she was already out in the sunlight, walking swiftly up the path. It was imperative that she get back as soon as possible, Mr. Brummell had explained. To allay suspicion and also to keep Mr. Ellicott from having a reason to come to the stable until such time as there would be nothing for him to find. Charlotte did not understand what was happening but she was determined to do as bid, for the order had come from the Regent via Mr. Brummell and as a loyal subject . . . It was nice to know that Mr. Forbes, too, was a loyal subject and that whatever he was doing was for the right cause. It was also nice to know, she realized, that he wanted to see her again, that he had apologized for his past behavior and that he seemed to like her. Until a few moments ago she would have told herself that what Mr. Rawley Forbes thought of her was immaterial, but now . . .

"Now, quickly, sir, your message." Brummell was all business once she was gone. Rawley repeated, as perfectly as he could, what Mr. Edward Delacour had told him. "I see," Brummell said. "Yes, well we know now for certain, don't we? I must advise you, Mr. Forbes, to say nothing of any of this to anyone. Your cousin . . . well, I hope that it will not cost him too much. As he is in no way involved—his business arrangements with the Marquis, it seems, are quite incidental. If you can let him know without giving even the slightest hint, that he had best cut his losses while he can, for the Kent-Chillinghams may be spending some time on the Continent in the next year or two. We were worried about you, too, you know. A little advice, man. You are too young for her and she would simply have used you. Take it from a somewhat experienced older man. Find yourself a young lady of quality and get married. Well, that is the pot advising the kettle, eh? But, still . . . Now you must away and swiftly, back to Newmarket I should think. You can say you got lost."

"But I must see—talk to Miss Linton."

"Oh, is that it, eh? A good choice. Again I seem to have underestimated you. Well, I can't help you here. But why not return to Linton Park? Spend the evening there. You'll be invited for the night."

"But she'll be here. . . ."

"How young and impetuous you are. She'll be home tomorrow, man. You can see her then."

Rawley felt himself getting angry. "Look, I've run your errand, did everything I was asked. Now I want to see her as soon as possible. Why can't I . . ."

"Come to the party? It would give everything away."

Rawley remembered that Delacour had originally suggested that he ride into Dunreath Manor as a suitor for Miss Linton.

"Not if I said I had come to woo Miss Linton, that I didn't care about protocol and . . ."

"You'd look an ass. Are you willing to look an ass?"

Rawley thought for a moment and then answered simply, "Yes."

"Well, it still won't do. I don't doubt your sincerity, but it would be too great a risk and too great an imposition on the young lady. Stay, I have an idea. What if you were to arrive *after* the Prince has slipped away? He and I will leave quietly after supper. No, that won't do. Another guest will arrive tonight. There will be too much confusion. I do not know why you cannot wait until tomorrow."

"Ellicott," Rawley answered. "Jack Ellicott."

Beau Brummell nodded his head. "Ah," he said, "now I understand."

The object of their immediate conversation was at that very moment striding across the lawn toward Charlotte, who had just appeared. Jack had been involved in several lengthy talks with the Regent and two other gentlemen he hardly knew and had, therefore, been prevented from doing what he had wished to do most: go to the stable and confront Rawley Forbes. If he hadn't known better, he told himself, he would have thought it was a conspiracy.

Now, however, he had finally freed himself from their various questions about Dunreath Manor, Suffolk, farming, hunting, and the like, questions his father could have answered far faster and far easier than himself, and he was determined to speak with Charlotte. More than that, he was determined that she accept his proposal of marriage.

She saw him coming, but there was no group nearby which she could join: Dunreath was far away talking with Cedric, her parents were almost as far, Aunt Judith was not to be seen, while Uncle George was with a group that included the Prince. There was nothing to do but face him, and from the look on his face, his wrath.

There were enough people close by, however, to keep him from yelling. He realized that he must not, under any circumstances, much as he might wish to do so, make a scene. And, so, although he was extremely angry and fearful, too, for most of his young adult life he had wanted Charlotte Linton and now things were happening that he could not control. He curbed his temper and attempted to change his grimace to a smile.

Charlotte remained calm but did not fully return his smile. She was not going to be put upon, not this day, not by Jack, not while she was thinking of Mr. Forbes and . . .

"Well, you've been there, I notice. Seen him. What did he want? No one sick at home or anything of the like?"

"Jack, you should not have read my private letter. Nor is what I have been doing any concern of yours. I have tried to tell you . . ."

"Wait. I . . . I apologize. About the letter. But what you do *is* my concern, Char. I have told you that I want to marry you . . . and . . . wait, please until I finish. I love you, have always loved you. This place, Dunreath Manor, all of it, which you love so much, shall be mine, ours someday. And, look, it will please my mother and father and Dunreath. Think of Dunreath, too. And *your* family. Char, it was meant to be."

"I don't know how to answer that, Jack."

"Say 'yes' and we'll make the announcement this minute. . . . The Prince . . ." Ellicott looked around, "wherever he has gone . . ."

"Jack, I can't say I'll marry you. I don't love you. I can't marry you now or ever." There, she had said it, if only he would accept it, if only he would.

"I can't believe that, Char. You're only seventeen, you don't know your own mind."

That angered her. "And you are nineteen! How well do you know your mind? This is . . ."

"I know that I have always wanted you . . . to marry you. . . ."

"But I don't want to marry *you*! And that is just as important."

"But Charlotte." He stopped. "It's that other fellow, that London rake you met, that Forbes."

She didn't, couldn't answer, though she knew that what he had guessed was probably so. Yet it wasn't her only reason, her best reason. Had there not been a Mr. Rawley Forbes, she knew she could never marry Jack Ellicott. Not for the sake of his family nor her own, not even for the sake of Dunreath.

"Where is he? Is he still there? I'll . . ."

"He's gone," she said, thinking that to be the truth, for she had seen Mr. Brummell just a minute before, slipping into the house from the rear.

"Where?"

"I don't know." I wish I did, she thought. "Now, I really must join the others, Jack. This is not seemly. And you should, too. I'm sorry about everything, but you must forget about me."

"I won't, Char. Never. I'll haunt you. I'll be here waiting and watching. You'll never escape me, Charlotte Linton." And, then, somehow he was gone and she was momentarily alone until joined by Dunreath who said, "My mother would like to see you, Char, in the house." She took Charlotte by the hand. "It's all right about Jack. Believe me, I understand. All of us do. Now come along."

Dunreath led her to the French doors that had been left open to let in the warm summer air, but did not follow her inside. When Charlotte's eyes adjusted to the sudden darkness, she saw that it was not her Aunt Judith standing there, but Mr. Beau Brummell and the Prince of Wales. There was another person there, too, she thought, on the far side and in the recesses of the large room, but she could not tell who it was. Perhaps it was her Aunt or her uncle, but she was not sure. Then she curtsied to the Prince and when she looked up the figure was gone.

"Ah, Miss Linton. I believe I must extend my gratitude for your help. It is too complicated to explain, but I am extremely grateful. So grateful that on Beau's advice, I have decided to repay the favor almost at once."

CHAPTER TWENTY

It was much later in the evening. Those who lived nearby and had no need to stay the night had left the party. Then, too, a certain important personage had left immediately after the evening meal had been served. With him had gone Mr. Brummell. The Lintons were staying the night as was their daughter, Charlotte. So was Cedric Fitzhugh. And it was he, who at this moment, was sitting next to Charlotte Linton in the drawing room where the gentlemen had joined the ladies as the festivities continued.

As usual, he stuttered when he spoke, but he kept his voice low and that plus the speech impediment would have made it impossible for anyone other than the young lady to whom he was speaking to understand what he said. Not that it mattered. No one was paying any special attention to them, although from time to time Jack Ellicott glowered from across the room.

"I . . . I have arranged ever . . . every . . . thing."

"I don't understand, Ceddy. I mean, I understand you, but what . . ."

"P P P Prinny. Asked me to."

"I see. All he said was that he would send me a message later and that I would be pleased by what the messenger brought. Are you the messenger, Ceddy?"

He nodded to her.

"What is the message, then? What have you brought? I really did nothing and I understand less. Are you—like Mr. Brummell?"

"Like the Beau? It wouldn't be possible." He hadn't stuttered, which surprised them both. "He's so . . . so . . . so . . . f f f fine."

"I meant, do you do things for the Prince?"

Ceddy looked away. It was a question, she understood, he would never answer directly.

For a while neither spoke and then she again asked him what message he had to deliver from the Regent.

"In . . . a . . . min . . . min . . . minute."

Long ago, as a small child, she had learned to trust Cedric Fitzhugh. She recalled that, as a little girl, when she would ask him for something he would either say "yes" or tell her why she could not have what she wanted. If the answer was positive, he always kept his word. But he never, no doubt because of his impediment, said more than he had to say. In a minute. Well, in roughly that time something would happen or he would do or say something more. She had only to wait and have faith in cousin Ceddy.

The conversations kept up around them and Charlotte heard them, yet she didn't, for whenever it happened that she was not directly involved with another person at the party, her mind harkened back to those few minutes in the stable and Rawley Forbes. What was different about them, about him, she wondered? Why had she so changed her opinion of him? She had always thought him good-looking, she supposed. But she had also thought him vain, arrogant, self-centered, a snob, a London snob. Was it because he was now in Suffolk? Was it because she had seen another side to him, the side that had not been shown before, the side that understood duty? Or, was it because he suddenly seemed interested in her in a wholly different way? At least she hoped he was. Perhaps, back in London, everything would revert to its original state and he would be telling her please not to meddle in his affairs, which she never had. Threatening to have her discharged and daring to embrace her on a whim!

That was what she remembered the most. It had been a shock, uncalled for, ungentlemanly; he should not have done it. Yet she remembered his lips almost tenderly.

"My d d d dear," Ceddy was saying, interrupting her thoughts, "you look . . . t t tired. Per . . . per . . . perhaps . . . you n n need some fr . . . fr . . . fresh air. Would you c c c care to stroll about the gar . . . gar . . . garden?"

Quizzically she answered, "Yes, if you should?" He didn't respond to the question in her voice, but instead took her hand and helped her up. It was doubtful that anyone noticed them leaving. No doubt that was why he had waited, had said "in a minute," meaning not a length of time, but until the time was right.

Quietly they left the room and moved out into the garden. There were one or two other strollers about, and although the moon was full, she could not see who they were. Gentlemen from the Prince's party, she suspected, a little bored by the country conversation. They moved in the shadows of the hedgerows and trees dotting the lawn.

Cedric, as was often the case with him, said nothing and she, although her mind had questions, was also silent. It was a beautiful night, his presence was comforting, and she could again without interruption think of Mr. Forbes.

Twice, three times around the garden; she *was* tired. She could hardly suppress a yawn. Was something supposed to happen? Why did he say nothing. Then she realized that he was watchful, that he had deliberately taken them a certain way to make sure . . . of what? That no one was skulking in the bushes? That . . .

"Ah, here . . . w w we are. J j j just per . . . fect, I be . . . lieve."

They were at the far end of the lawn, away from the house, near the path to the stables. The other strollers were not in evidence. They were alone until she looked up and there, almost miraculously, materialized the very vision she had been having. He stood there, shyly, diffident, still in hunting attire, silhouetted by the moon.

The Prince said I would be pleased by what the messenger brought. Are you the messenger, Ceddy? The words ran through her brain, then she was in a recess, shaded by a great tree and Cedric was gone, striding swiftly across the lawn, and Rawley Forbes reached out his hand and took hers and she could tell that they both were shaking.

"Miss Linton," he said.

"Mr. Forbes," was all she could answer.

"Miss Linton?"

"Yes?"

"I don't know . . . I don't know a number of things. That is obvious. I can explain very little about this afternoon. Only to say that what I did was a matter of state and I have been told that I must not ever tell anyone. Mr. Delacour—and then Mr. Brummell—have sworn me to secrecy. I can only say that the two of them . . . are engaged in helping the Regent through a difficult time and the message I brought was for him."

"Mr. Brummell told me that." She did not reply that she, too, had a secret, that she knew a third party, Ceddy, who was also engaged in helping the Prince Regent through a difficult time.

"I thought he would. But . . ."

"Yes?"

"That is not the only reason I am here. I mean . . . oh, I don't know where to begin. I have been such a fool. Mr. Brummell asked me . . . I wanted to come to see you tonight and he asked me if I were willing to seem an ass, arriving out of the blue, uninvited, in my hunting attire . . . and . . . and I said, yes, I would be willing because it was importantt o me that I see you . . . as soon as possible. You see, Miss Linton . . . oh, I am miserable . . ."

"Do not be. I am pleased that you wished to see me . . . tonight. I am pleased that you are here."

"You are? Oh, I say . . . listen, how can I explain myself. I treated you badly in London. You must know, I am not all I pretend. I am a nobody. If James had not taken Angelique and myself in, had not adopted us, I would be someone's 'prentice, no doubt. I am so much less than you, than all of them. But I wanted to rise above my station. James made it possible. He has been very good to me. He and Valerie, well you must not judge them too harshly. . . ."

"Judge them? I am very fond of them both."

"Are you? Oh, good. Well, as I was saying about myself, I am a nobody. I have tried to be like the others. I have tried to play the dandy, the rake, and in doing so I have alienated the very one . . . Oh, Miss Linton, can you ever forgive me?"

"Sir, there is nothing to forgive. And I care not for station in life. I am not royalty after all. Here in Suffolk, we are considered gentry and we have more than most, I suppose, but I was and am working for your cousin because of the money as well as other things. To me it is important what a person does, how he behaves, what his ideals are . . . not how much money or how much in society he is. I care not a fig for what you were, Mr. Forbes. Only for what you are."

"Really? I am so glad. I promise I shall change if you

will allow me . . . If you want me to change . . . and will allow me to . . . to see you. Let me explain my haste. You see, I understood . . . I saw certain things and I was afraid that if I did not speak now, at once, that you might promise yourself. . . . Oh, I am making such a botch of this. I have spent years, it would seem, affecting indifference and then when it is necessary to be sincere and to tell you how much, to tell you everything, I cannot find the right words. Please, Miss Linton, I beg of you, do not allow yourself to become betrothed to Mr. Ellicott. Give me a chance to redeem myself. If I cannot, I shall be the most miserable of men. There, I have said it, why it was urgent that I see you tonight, why I am foolishly here uninvited. I don't know why Mr. Brummell allowed me to stay except that I told him that I was anxious, that I wanted at least to speak with you. If you are to marry Mr. Ellicott, so be it. But I wanted at least first to let you know my intentions . . . Oh, Miss Linton, is it possible, could you . . . ever . . . care for me? Would you marry me, Miss Linton?"

He almost yelled the last words and she looked around, afraid that others might have heard, but the garden was still. Cedric had, as he had promised, arranged everything at the behest of the Regent. And now . . .

"Mr. Forbes, I can hardly speak. I don't know how to answer you at this time. First, though, let me put your mind at ease. I have no intention of marrying Mr. Ellicott, although he has, indeed, tendered his affections to me and asked for my hand. I have told him that I cannot marry him, Sir."

She heard a sigh—of relief?—almost as loud as his proposal. Although she knew he could barely see her, she put her fingers to his lips. "Sh."

"Oh, Miss Linton," he whispered, "you have made me the happiest of men. If you will allow me but to see you . . . here and in London . . . ?"

"Mr. Forbes," she replied, surprised that she could ever be so forward, "nothing would please me more."

Then she found herself in his arms and he kissed her over and over again, gently and timidly at first and then passionately, until she felt her body quivering in his embrace.

It was the sound that stopped the embrace, the quiet "ahem" that told them that someone was nearby and wished to interrupt them, but delicately. Embarrassed she stepped back from his arms and looked about, but the moon, which had fortuitously hidden behind a cloud, to bathe their kisses in darkness, remained there. Still, someone had seen them, was close to them.

"I . . . I . . . think . . . ev . . . everything is un . . . un . . . un . . . der con . . . control. By . . . by . . . by that I m . . . m . . . ean there is nothing to wor . . . wor . . . worry about. But, Charlotte, you . . . you . . . you . . . should come in . . . in . . . inside now."

Rawley spoke. "The plan?"

"Suc . . . suc . . . succeeded. Best to for . . . for . . . forget it all now. Bo . . . bo . . . both of you."

"Then I should be going," Rawley said, "much as I hate to leave."

"No," Charlotte said, suddenly afraid that she would not see him again. "The road at night . . . It will be too dark to ride and too long a trip."

"Then I shall sleep in the stable and leave before daybreak."

"Where will you . . . ?"

"To Linton Park. I must return the horse, for one thing."

"Will you wait until we return?"

"Later in the day? Yes, for I shall wish to speak to your father. I only wish that I weren't still in these clothes."

"They are clothes my father will respect even more than . . . well, in London garb he would not know what to think."

"Then I will bathe, at least. I doubt that he would appreciate a totally unkempt man asking for his eldest daughter's hand."

Cedric Fitzhugh chuckled. "Pr . . . Prinny will be pl . . . pleased."

"I shall always be grateful to him," Rawley said.

"We both shall," Charlotte added. "And to you, dear coz. You have been most helpful. But, as you say, we must go in. I am so happy and I can say nothing, not while I am here." She was, of course, thinking of Jack. She wanted to tell Dunreath, her mother and father, to shout it out, but it would be best if she remained silent until they were back at Linton Park. After Rawley had spoken to her father, after everything was agreed upon, then she would write to Jack.

She would be going back to London. She hoped it would not be a long engagement.

"I shall be thinking of you on my bed of straw," Rawley said.

"Until tomorrow, then." She curtsied and he bowed.

Cedric, looking on benignly, had some thoughts, too. The Prince's position was now secure. Kent-Chillingham was returning to London on the morrow. From there he would be going to the Continent with his wife for an extended stay, as had been suggested. The important person, the representative of the Earl of Liverpool, had been stopped short of Dunreath Manor and apprised of the situation. He had decided to continue onto the Bury St. Edmonds. Spencer Perceval had been, in a sense, routed. He would remain Prime Minister, but not for as much as a year longer. The power would pass and the Regent would be given free reign to govern the country. There was only one problem. How well would he govern once he achieved his aims? Well, Cedric thought, it was a chance that had to be taken. For as long as the King lived, there would have been a madman at the helm. And the ship of state could not afford that in these perilous times.

But what did these two young people standing near him in the dark, no doubt gazing fondly at one another, wishing that he was not here, understand of that. It was just as well. Politics were for people such as himself. Confirmed bachelors. Love was for the young and impetuous.

Gently he reached out and touched Charlotte's sleeve. Imperceptibly she nodded and took his arm. Rawley Forbes sighed and slipped away in the dark, to his "bed of straw."

It was a good night's work, Cedric thought as he and Charlotte started back toward the house. Soon his cousin would be engaged. He could remember her as a little girl. How quickly they grow. Before he knew it he would be an uncle. He smiled at the thought.

The moon, so long hidden, reappeared as they walked across the wide lawn of Dunreath Manor. Charlotte stopped and looked back at the tree, hoping . . . but Cedric, who had also turned, could tell that he was gone. But he would be nearby, she understood that.

Charlotte saw him smiling, shyly smiled in return.

"Thank you, Ceddy. All my life I shall bless you."

So that he would not stutter, he took time to form all the

words in his head. It was something he wanted to say simply, but clearly.

"I think," he said, "even Mother will be pleased."

Charlotte nodded. As they came to the French doors and she could hear the continuing sounds of conversation, she thought of Anne, her sister. Anne's prediction had been right.

Within a year—no, if she had her way, before the year was out—she would be marrying a London man.

Charlotte sighed. Anne, too, would be marrying one day. And then Caroline . . . all of them. And perhaps Arthur and Dunreath. She hoped so. If only Dunreath could feel the same happiness she was now feeling.

I'm grown up, she told herself. I have changed. I shall be wed. Everything will be different. For a moment she felt sad. But, then, she told herself, like the seasons, everything had to change.

She would have a new life. But she was not leaving the old one. Her family would always be there. From London she would come home to visit as often as possible. The Lintons might, one by one, leave home, but their hearts—or a part of their hearts—would always remain behind.

Linton Park would always be there.

Secure in her knowledge and in her new-found happiness, she walked boldly into the drawing room. Dunreath came to her and held out her arms.

"Charlotte," she said and embraced her cousin.

"Oh, Dunreath, I am so happy! Isn't the world a beautiful place? Today has been the most perfect day of my life."

ASTON HALL ROMANCES

From Pinnacle Books

Wholesome and sophisticated stories about modern women facing modern dilemmas— written especially for women like you!

☐ **41-117-0 A DISTANT SONG #105**
by Iris Bromige
Sarah is torn between the man she loves and the fear she is being used.

☐ **41-118-9 STARFIRE #106**
by Arlene Morgan
Only a secret she can never reveal stands between Peggy and the man she loves.

☐ **41-119-7 DOCTORS IN LOVE #107**
by Sonia Deane
Emma is a doctor whose handsome medical partner wants to mix business with pleasure.

☐ **41-120-0 NO STARS SO BRIGHT #108**
by Mary Faid
Cathy's love for Neil overpowers everything but the barrier between them.

☐ **41-121-9 THE SCENT OF ROSEMARY #109**
by Lorna Hill
For Ellie and the young doctor it's only a holiday affair...until fate intervenes and throws them together again.

☐ **41-122-7 SHETLAND SUMMER #110**
by Audrie Manley-Tucker
Serena is torn between an attractive widower and her handsome employer.

All Books $1.50
Buy them at your local bookstore or use this handy coupon.
Clip and mail this page with your order

**PINNACLE BOOKS, INC.—Reader Service Dept.
271 Madison Ave., New York, NY 10016**

Please send me the book(s) I have checked above. I am enclosing $_____ (please add 75¢ to cover postage and handling). Send check or money order only—no cash or C.O.D.'s.

Mr./Mrs./Miss _____

Address _____

City _____ State/Zip _____

Please allow six weeks for delivery. Prices subject to change without notice.

The Quotable Woman

1800–the present

compiled and edited by Elaine Partnow

"Both an indispensable reference tool—and a book to dip into and enjoy."
— *Working Woman* magazine

Timeless. Poignant. Entertaining. Now, for the first time in paperback, two unique encyclopedic volumes exclusively devoted to the insights, contemplations and inspirations of over 1300 women—from suffragists to liberationists, authors to educators—that no woman should be without!

- ☐ 40-859-5 *VOLUME ONE: 1800–1899* $3.95
- ☐ 40-874-9 *VOLUME TWO: 1900–the present* $3.95

And.. *THE QUOTABLE WOMAN* box set—an ideal gift!

- ☐ 41-050-6 *VOLUMES ONE* and *TWO* $7.90

Buy them at your local bookstore or use this handy coupon.
Clip and mail this page with your order

PINNACLE BOOKS, INC.—Reader Service Dept.
271 Madison Ave., New York, NY 10016

Please send me the book(s) I have checked above. I am enclosing $_____ (please add 75¢ to cover postage and handling). Send check or money order only—no cash or C.O.D.'s.

Mr./Mrs./Miss _____

Address _____

City _____ State/Zip _____

Please allow six weeks for delivery. Prices subject to change without notice.

Melissa Hepburne

Over one million copies in print!

☐ **40-329-1 PASSION'S PROUD CAPTIVE** $2.25
Did Lancelot Savage save Jennifer VanDerLinde from a crew of lecherous sailors just to have her for himself? Deep in her heart, she knew that she did not want to extinguish the blazing inferno inside her. But when Savage is accused of piracy and treason, she must submit to the perverse pleasures of the man she despises most to set free her beloved.

☐ **40-471-9 PASSION'S SWEET SACRIFICE** $2.50
As World War I erupts in fury, the devastatingly beautiful Sabrina St. Claire is pursued by the richest, most powerful men in all of Europe. But when fate thrusts her at the mercy of a cruel German general and his despicable officers, she must submit to their unspeakable depravities in order to save the only man she will ever love.

☐ **40-654-1 PASSION'S BLAZING TRIUMPH** $2.50
Amidst the raging frenzy of the French Revolution, beautiful Isabella VanDerLinde Jones—deposed empress of an exotic Mediterranean island—must choose between the dashing D'Arcy Calhoun and the one man who can save him: General Napoleon Bonaparte.

Buy them at your local bookstore or use this handy coupon.
Clip and mail this page with your order

PINNACLE BOOKS, INC.—Reader Service Dept.
271 Madison Ave., New York, NY 10016

Please send me the book(s) I have checked above. I am enclosing $_____ (please add 75¢ to cover postage and handling). Send check or money order only—no cash or C.O.D.'s.

Mr./Mrs./Miss _____

Address _____

City _____ State/Zip _____

Please allow six weeks for delivery. Prices subject to change without notice.

Patricia Matthews

**...an unmatched sensuality, tenderness and passion.
No wonder there are over 15,000,000 copies in print!**

☐ **40-644-4 LOVE, FOREVER MORE** $2.50
The tumultuous story of spirited Serena Foster and her determination to survive the raw, untamed West.

☐ **40-646-0 LOVE'S AVENGING HEART** $2.50
Life with her brutal stepfather in colonial Williamsburg was cruel, but Hannah McCambridge would survive—and learn to love with a consuming passion.

☐ **40-645-2 LOVE'S DARING DREAM** $2.50
The turbulent story of indomitable Maggie Donnevan, who fled the poverty of Ireland to begin a new life in the American Northwest.

☐ **40-658-4 LOVE'S GOLDEN DESTINY** $2.50
It was a lust for gold that brought Belinda Lee together with three men in the Klondike gold rush, only to be trapped by the wildest of passions.

☐ **40-395-X LOVE'S MAGIC MOMENT** $2.50
Evil and ecstasy are entwined in the steaming jungles of Mexico, where Meredith Longley searches for a lost city but finds greed, lust, and seduction.

☐ **40-394-1 LOVE'S PAGAN HEART** $2.50
An exquisite Hawaiian princess is torn between love for her homeland and the only man who can tame her pagan heart.

☐ **40-659-2 LOVE'S RAGING TIDE** $2.50
Melissa Huntoon seethed with humiliation as her ancestral plantation home was auctioned away, suddenly vulnerable to the greed and lust of a man's world.

☐ **40-660-6 LOVE'S SWEET AGONY** $2.75
Amid the colorful world of thoroughbred farms that gave birth to the first Kentucky Derby, Rebecca Hawkins learns that horses are more easily handled than men.

☐ **40-647-9 LOVE'S WILDEST PROMISE** $2.50
Abducted aboard a ship bound for the Colonies, innocent Sarah Moody faces a dark voyage of violence and unbridled lust.

☐ **40-721-1 LOVE'S MANY FACES (Poems)** $1.95
Poems of passion, humor and understanding that exquisitely capture that special moment, that wonderful feeling called love.

Buy them at your local bookstore or use this handy coupon:
Clip and mail this page with your order

**PINNACLE BOOKS, INC.—Reader Service Dept.
271 Madison Ave., New York, NY 10016**

Please send me the book(s) I have checked above. I am enclosing $_____ (please add 75¢ to cover postage and handling). Send check or money order only—no cash or C.O.D.'s.

Mr./Mrs./Miss _____

Address _____

City _____ State/Zip _____

Please allow six weeks for delivery. Prices subject to change without notice.

Paula Fairman

Romantic intrigue at its finest—
over 2,500,000 copies in print!

☐ **40-105-1 FORBIDDEN DESTINY** $1.95
A helpless stowaway aboard the whaling ship *Gray Ghost*, Kate McCrae was in no position to refuse the lecherous advances of Captain Steele.

☐ **40-569-3 THE FURY AND THE PASSION** $2.50
From the glitter of Denver society to the lawlessness of the wild West, Stacey Pendarrow stalks the trail of her elusive lover for one reason: to kill him.

☐ **40-181-7 IN SAVAGE SPLENDOR** $2.25
Torn between fierce loyalty to an agent of King George III and a desperate hunger for an Irish rogue, Charity Varney knew she would trade a lifetime of security for one night of savage splendor.

☐ **40-697-5 PORTS OF PASSION** $2.50
Abducted aboard the *Morning Star*, heiress Kristen Chalmers must come to terms not only with immediate danger, but the desperate awakening of her own carnal desires.

☐ **40-474-3 STORM OF DESIRE** $2.25
The only woman in a rough and brutal railroad camp in the wild Southwest, young Reesa Flowers becomes enmeshed in a web of greed, sabotage, and lust.

☐ **41-006-9 THE TENDER AND THE SAVAGE** $2.75
In the wild and ravaged plains of the Dakota Territory, beautiful young Crimson Royale is torn between her savage lust for a Sioux Indian and her tender desires for his worst enemy—a captain in Custer's Army.

Buy them at your local bookstore or use this handy coupon.
Clip and mail this page with your order

PINNACLE BOOKS, INC.—Reader Service Dept.
271 Madison Ave., New York, NY 10016

Please send me the book(s) I have checked above. I am enclosing $_____ (please add 75¢ to cover postage and handling). Send check or money order only—no cash or C.O.D.'s.

Mr./Mrs./Miss _____

Address _____

City _____ State/Zip _____

Please allow six weeks for delivery. Prices subject to change without notice.

The Windhaven Saga
by Marie de Jourlet

Over 4,000,000 copies in print!

☐ **40-642-8 WINDHAVEN PLANTATION** $2.50
The epic novel of the Bouchard family, who dared to cross the boundaries of society and create a bold new heritage.

☐ **40-643-6 STORM OVER WINDHAVEN** $2.50
Windhaven Plantation and the Bouchard dream are shaken to their very roots in this torrid story of men and women driven by ambition and damned by desire.

☐ **41-267-3 LEGACY OF WINDHAVEN** $2.75
After the Civil War the Bouchards move west to Texas—a rugged, untamed land where they must battle Indians, bandits and cattle rustlers to insure the legacy of Windhaven.

☐ **40-348-8 RETURN TO WINDHAVEN** $2.50
Amid the turbulent Reconstruction years, the determined Bouchards fight to hold on to Windhaven Range while struggling to regain an old but never forgotten plantation.

☐ **41-258-4 WINDHAVEN'S PERIL** $2.75
Luke Bouchard and his family launch a new life at Windhaven Plantation—but the past returns to haunt them.

☐ **40-722-X TRIALS OF WINDHAVEN** $2.75
Luke and Laure Bouchard face their most bitter trial yet, as their joyful life at Windhaven Plantation is threatened by an unscrupulous carpetbagger.

Buy them at your local bookstore or use this handy coupon.
Clip and mail this page with your order

PINNACLE BOOKS, INC.—Reader Service Dept.
271 Madison Ave., New York, NY 10016

Please send me the book(s) I have checked above. I am enclosing $_____ (please add 75¢ to cover postage and handling). Send check or money order only—no cash or C.O.D.'s.

Mr./Mrs./Miss _____

Address _____

City _____ State/Zip _____

Please allow six weeks for delivery. Prices subject to change without notice.